Mam
(Book 1

MW01113836

By Michelle Stimpson

Published by Michelle Stimpson

For all the women of God

who minister as a way of life.

Great is your reward.

Acknowledgments

Always, thanks be to God for the life given to me in Christ. The more You reveal Yourself to me, the more I realize what You have already done for and through me. You alone are amazing!

I'm thankful for my writing group members who gave me encouragement and feedback throughout the drafting of this book: Janice, Lynne, Kellie, Jane, Margie, the two Patty's, Kesha, Jackie, Lyndie and everyone else who dropped by for either critique or food. You ladies are so much fun!

Monica Harris-Mindolovich, your editorial eye is always a blessing to me. And special thanks to Vicki Prather for the second polishing.

Thanks to my family for your unyielding support. I know it can be hard living with an artist. I believe you all are graced to put up with me.

Kimberly, thanks for giving me all this advice about cooking with turkey. Thanks to Kimmie McNeese for giving me the scoop on how churches operate. And also thanks to one of my real-life Mama B's, fellow writer Ginnie Bivona, who gave me the "Rule of One" and continues to amaze me with her spunk at the ripe young age of 81. To the original Mama B in my life, my grandmother – thanks for making the resolution of this book clear to me in one word of wisdom.

I'm completely humbled by the book clubs and individual readers who continue to read my works after all these years. It is my hope that we have grown in

Him together. And it is my pleasure to continue to serve you through books and characters and messages that (I trust) encourage your faith. Thank you, thank you, thank you.

To God Be the Glory!

Chapter 1

If Rev. Omar hollers one more time that it's gonna be hotter than this in hell, I'm going to have to walk out of this sanctuary. I, for one, don't plan on spending no time in hell. No sense in gettin' prepared for a place you ain't goin' to.

I kept my feet still, though. He was trying, bless his heart. And it wasn't his fault somebody stole all the copper out the church's air conditioning system the night before. People ought to have more respect for the house of God. But I guess when some folks get broke and their babies start crying for milk, don't matter to them how they get the money so long as they get it.

I'd already asked the Lord to touch the rascal who took the copper; give him a mind to work an honest job and let somebody hire him. Either that or put him in jail so he can't mess up nobody else's air.

Rev. Martin said the thief was probably somebody on drugs who needed quick money. "All these Dallas folks movin' into town," he had fussed earlier while we rummaged through the storage looking for fans and Kleenexes before the service started. "They bring the dope and the crime problems with 'em."

"You sure right about that," Mother Ophelia Pugh seconded. "I wish they'd find some place else to move. Peasner gettin' way too crowded for me."

"Where else you want 'em to go?" I laughed quietly.

"I don't know, Beatrice, just not here."

Peasner had always been a good spot to live. Folk got along with each other, for the most part. We was close enough to the city to have a good doctor and mighty fine shopping; far enough out to not need an alarm system for your house. People still knew each other—families, businesses and whatnot. At least that's the way it used to be. But since they put that highway loop through Peasner, seem like a whole lot of restaurants poppin' up. New houses going up so fast, make your head swim.

Ophelia passed me another unopened tissue box. These would come in handy when folks got to sweating. "Sister, I like that suit. Sharp! Tell you what, B, if I lose about fifty pounds, I'mma have to come make my home in your closet."

I shooed at her. "Please, Ophelia. You know as well as I do, they make pretty clothes for all sizes. Not like back when all you could buy was a muumuu, over size fourteen."

Ophelia pulled the light switch and stepped down off the stool. "That's it. No more Kleenexes."

I looked down at the four boxes in my hand and shook my head. The church had nine pews on each side. On a regular Sunday, all but the last couple of rows would be at least half full. I figured once folks got to standing and clapping and carrying on, we'd need a whole lot more than those few tissues and funeral home fans to keep them from passing out.

Now back in my day, before we had air conditioning, we could worship the Lord all day at church with just the breezes flowing through the open windows. We were used to high temperatures. I do believe God graced us for the Texas heat before He let us figure out how to beat it.

Don't get me wrong, though, I likes my air conditioner. My late husband, Albert, used to fuss—ooh, Lord, that man could fuss—about me running the air twenty-four hours a day. We never could agree on what degrees the house should be.

I sure do miss fussin' with Albert.

Well, anyway, I already knew those folk sure would be fussin' that Sunday. Had to go on and get my mind ready for it. And get myself ready, too. My no-air-conditioning days were long behind me. At seventy-two years old, I had no business letting my body get overheated. If service went too long, I would have to tip out.

"I don't know, Mama B." Rev. Martin had sighed, wiping sweat from his forehead already. He led us from the fellowship hall back to the main foyer. "You think we ought to cancel service? It'll start getting real hot around noon."

Mother Pugh shook her head so hard her pillbox hat like ta fell off. "We will do no such thing. This church been open every Sunday for thirty-nine years. We don't cancel service for nothin'. If the flood of '87 didn't stop us, neither will a little sunshine."

"Who's preachin' today?" I had asked him.

His eyes shifted off to the right a little, then he replied. "I believe Rev. Omar, from St. Luke."

Rev. Martin's face winced a bit. I knew he was suffering, trying to run things in his uncle's absence and his aunt's illness. Our Pastor, Ed Phillips, was hit-and-miss on Sundays since they took first lady Geneva Phillips to get special treatment at that cancer center in Oklahoma.

"How's Geneva?"

His eyebrows raised, he shook his head. "Mama B, I really don't know. Uncle Ed says she's entering stage four."

In all my years, I done heard so many doctors be wrong, terms like "stage four" don't phase me none. "Rev. Martin, don't you be moved by what they say, you keep your aunt lifted in prayer."

"Yes, ma'am."

I looked up at Rev. Martin. Spittin' image of his mother – I used to work with her in the salon. Rev. Martin was still young. In his early fifties. Needed to prove himself a faithful Indian before he took on the title of Chief one of these days—if the Lord ever called him to preach.

Ophelia, Rev. Martin and I entered the sanctuary again through the swinging wooden doors. I took a deep breath. Lord knows I love the smell of His house. The carpet, the pews, the old wooden pulpit Pastor Phillips and my Albert built with their own hands. They set every stained glass window in place, nailed down every pew, laid all the baseboards on top of the carpet. Pastor Phillips wasn't married back then, so I had to look out for both of them. Brought them iced tea and lemonade, fed them after the end of a hard day's work—mostly on Saturdays and Sundays because we all had full-time jobs. Took us a while, but Mt. Zion had been built with a lot of faith, patience, love, and sweat.

Back in '73, when Albert and I donated the other half of our property to build the church on, we knew this space would be something special. A place where folks could come and get help and experience the love of Jesus through His people.

Pastor Phillips really wasn't that good a preacher back then. He used to read from his yellow legal pad like my kids used to read from their little note cards when they gave a speech at school. Nervous! But God anointed Pastor Phillips and used him anyway because he had a willing heart and he loved people. He was a real good pastor before he was a real good preacher. Sometimes, it's like that. God give you grace as you go in faith.

Anyhow, we sure did miss Pastor Phillips' pastorin' and his preachin' while he was out caring for his wife. Rev. Martin was doing a good enough job of holding down the fort, but all those different ministers coming on all those different Sundays was startin' to wear me out. Some of 'em so wired up, felt like we was at a rock and roll show. And some of 'em be 'bout to put me to sleep right there on the front row. I know the Lord just trainin' 'em up like he did Pastor Phillips. I got to be more patient.

But wasn't going to be much patience that day with no air in the building. Already, I could feel my pores opening up, and it wasn't even nine o'clock yet.

I looked at Rev. Martin over the rim of my glasses. "Listen here, I'll pray and ask the Lord to hold off the heat. You tell Rev. Omar to preach real fast today, okay?"

Chapter 2

"Let the church say…"

"Amen."

My feet took off toward the doorway. *Father forgive me for rushing out of Your house, but we need to get this copper back first thing in the morning!*

The only fellowshipping I did after the benediction was with Angela Freeholt, our church secretary. Poor child must not have gotten the word that the church would be hot. She had on an unseasonable black, long-sleeved dress with stockings and closed-toe shoes.

"Angela, I just want to make sure you have all the numbers you need to call the insurance company tomorrow. If not, you can get 'em from Rev. Martin, need be."

She wiped moisture from under her glasses and nodded as we both crossed the church threshold and entered the sunlight. Same temperature outside as it was inside. "Yes, Mama B. I've got them."

"Okay. And if you need to sit in the cool of my house while you talk to 'em, just come on through."

She slowed for a second to give me a genuine thank-you. "We may need to do that, hot as it is out here. You take care. Stay out of this heat."

"You know I will," I assured her. "You have a blessed week."

"Same to you."

With the insurance business well under way, I booked it on across the church lawn, passed through the gate, and entered my own back yard. All my flowers seemed to be hiding. "Where y'all at?" I whispered to them. You got to talk to plants and flowers, you know?

When my kids were little, we had a swing set in the back yard. And a couple of dogs—Blackie was Son's dog (that's what we call Albert, Jr.); Co-Co was Otha's. Wish I had a dollar for all the scrapes and cuts and fights my two sons got playing outside. My two girls played and fought, too, except Cassandra was a tattletale. She always ran inside to tell me they was fighting the minute she started losing. And Debra Kay would come inside when she got a little dirt on her pants. She never was one for getting all messy. Takes after her momma.

Soon as everybody moved out, Albert and I pulled up the swing, filled in all the holes the dogs had dug, and turned the back yard into a little piece of heaven. Well, I shouldn't say Albert and *I* did it 'cause mostly it was him.

He'd been gone for almost eight years and I didn't have a mind to keep it up like he did. Got me a yardman to come out and cut the grass every couple of weeks. Didn't plant no more flowers, though. Whatever flowers I had just shot up out the ground and surprised me whenever they got good and ready.

Made me feel like Albert was still giving me flowers.

Concrete stepping stones led me another fifty feet, through the grass and up to my back porch. Few months earlier, Son had advised me to start locking my back door. I had agreed because I didn't want to hear him fuss, but every time I had to fish my key out of my purse, I wished I hadn't. Especially not that day, when my throat was screaming for a glass of iced water.

Finally, I found my key and let myself in the back door. *Thank You, Lord.* The cool rush of conditioned air welcomed me home along with the smell of onions and other vegetables simmering in my crock pot.

One good thing about living alone is you don't have to worry about what other folk want to eat. You feel like eatin' turkey stew in June, you eat turkey stew in June. Nobody there to complain they don't want a winter meal on a summer day.

One more good thing about being by myself: I still had a good portion left of the chocolate cake I made Friday. Ooh wee! My kids and my husband used to tear through a cake in less than twenty-four hours. Now, it's all mine. Took so long to eat it sometimes I walked over to the church and gave part of it to the children's choir when they finish rehearsing. Better to give it away than be wasteful.

The screen door swatted my behind and I shut as well as locked the door behind me. Son would have been proud.

Walked through the kitchen, making sure everything was in place. Didn't expect no problems, just habit, I guess.

The den's wood-paneled walls were *my* family wall of fame. All four of my kids' high school graduation pictures, Son's military picture, mine and Albert's graduation and a shot of us standing beside our wedding cake, too. I know people on the decorating channels don't hardly put photographs on their walls no more. I feel sorry for 'em. Covered all up with wallpaper or just plain old white paint to make it look "clean". Hmph. Clean and lonely-lookin' if you ask me.

The kitchen and dining area, off to the right, brought in all the sunlight. Plenty good cookin' and good times in there.

Three bedrooms all down the left hallway. One bathroom there, too. Kids used to fight over that bathroom something awful! Albert and I had our own bathroom in the master suite. We added that in '78 because soon as Debra Kay hit the teenage years, I knew for sure I couldn't share a bathroom with her. Take her thirty minutes just to put her hair in a ponytail.

All the back part of the house was just as I'd left it. Last thing to do was walk through the front parlor. Nobody ever went in the room, but every once in a while somebody would slip a prayer request or a thank-you note through the mailbox and I'd find it laying there on my floor.

A quick look through the front room showed me something more than a little card had arrived for me that day.

Chapter 3

Through the sheer part of my curtains, I could see two figures sitting on my porch bench. A woman and a little boy. I paused for a second, had to think of who they might be.

Then I caught onto her voice as she fussed at the child. "Cameron, this is the last time I'm going to tell you to tie your shoes correctly. You don't want Mama B to think you eight years old and can't even tie your shoes right, do you?"

"No ma'am."

Cameron. Nikki. I should have known something was going on with those two as much as the Lord had been bringing them up in my Spirit. My mind didn't even have time to ask the questions before I found myself outside again, on that porch hugging them.

"Mama B," she nearly cried as she pulled me into her embrace, "I'm so glad to see you."

"Me, too, Nikki-Nik!" Inside, my heart was bubbling over with joy. Nikki, my oldest grandbaby, come to Peasner to see me.

"And look at you, Cameron! Oh, you look so much like your grandfather, it's a shame!"

He didn't say anything, just stood there with a little shy smile on his face.

My granddaughter looked good. Like she'd been taking care of herself. Light brown skin, just like her Daddy, button nose like her mother. Got the kind of hair can straighten out with just a blow dryer. Toes done, nails done. Been taking care of herself.

Cameron looked well, too, though he was still holding on to quite a bit of baby fat. No matter, I'd rather have him too plump than too skinny any day. *Thank You, Lord, for keeping them in Your care.*

After all our greeting, I took a step back from them. "Does your father know you're here?"

She smacked her lips, whispered so Cameron wouldn't hear us. "Mama B, you know my daddy don't talk to me."

Son said the same thing about her. I could tell Nikki didn't really want to talk about her father. "How's your mother?"

Her face smoothed back out again. "She's fine. You know my Momma—off seeing the world. She went on a cruise with some of her friends to celebrate their fiftieth birthdays."

"She know you're here?"

"Yes, ma'am."

I glanced behind Nikki and saw four bulging suitcases parked on my wooden porch planks.

"Sweetie, you planning on staying in Peasner for a spell?"

She looked up at me with her slanted, brown eyes—same as my husband's and her father's. Real fast, she darted those eyes away from me. "Mama B, I'm in a really bad situation right now. We need to stay with you...for just a little while."

Freeze.

I done heard *that* one plenty of times before. Peoples evicted for not paying rent, wives leavin' their cheatin' husbands, teenagers not getting along with their parents. Every time, I listen. Wait for the Holy Spirit to tell me what to do because I don't want to call myself trying to help somebody, but end up hindering what God really wants to do in their life. Some folk need a few good homeless, hungry, sleepless nights to make the voice of God real clear. Other folk need a soft bed and a warm meal before they can hear Him. He knows, and He has to let me know, too.

Now, I have to be honest and say the first thing came to my mind wasn't nothin' from the Lord. I was thinking about me and all the stuff I didn't want to have to put up with like an eight-year-old running around my house and a twenty-something year-old doing whatever it is they do. Share my TV. Plus I gotta cook for three now. I know Nikki old enough to cook for herself, but I might as well go ahead and cook for everybody long as I'm in the kitchen already.

What else? Gotta wait for some more hot water before I take my shower. Water bill, power bill, gas bill higher.

All this is coming from me, now, and I'm waiting on the Holy Spirit to agree with my thoughts. He didn't. And since the Lord didn't co-sign on my veto, I had no choice except to put myself aside; wait until He say something different. Wasn't for Him and Albert's life insurance, I wouldn't have a place to rest my head, either. *Thank You, Lord, for a home that I can share.*

Unfreeze.

"You and Cameron get those suitcases and come on in here. I've got something for us to eat all ready."

"Thank you, Mama B."

I should have known the first words out of Cameron's mouth would be pertaining to food. "What'd you cook?"

"Turkey stew."

He had the nerve to draw up his face. "Turkey stew?"

"Yes, sir, with lots of vegetables. Chocolate cake for dessert."

A big smile spread across his chubby little face; cheeks just begging for a kiss and a pinch. "I like chocolate cake."

I can tell. "Only after you finish your stew."

At my word, they followed me to Debra Kay and Cassandra's old bedroom. Since I mentioned dessert, apparently Cameron became my best friend. "Mama B," he said, breathing hard as he rolled suitcases down the hallway, "does the cake have frosting?"

"Sure does. Chocolate on chocolate." Wouldn't be no extra food to give away so long as he was around.

After they set down their suitcases, we all washed up and met at the kitchen table to eat. I blessed the food and asked the Lord to make Nikki's time with me profitable for His sake. We all said, "Amen" and started eating.

I love my grands, but letting people move in with you always bring some kinda problem. Might be a big problem, might be a little problem. But it's always a problem, that's for sure.

Chapter 4

Angela Freeholt took me up on my offer and come knocking on the door at eight-thirty the next morning. I could tell by the look on her face something wasn't right.

"Y'all come on in," I said, holding the screen door open for them. Seein' as this was business, I switched on my proper, professional words. "Would you like some tea?"

"Oh, no ma'am." The gentleman, wearing a white button-down shirt and a pair of khaki pants, sat on the edge of the love seat. Obvious to me, he didn't plan on being in my house too long.

Angela sat next to me on the couch. "Mr. Colbert, this is Mrs. Beatrice Jackson. Like I said, she's a church mother. Do you mind telling her what you told me?"

"Nice to meet you, Mrs. Jackson. And you can call me Dustin."

He raised his behind off the chair a tad so he could lean over and shake my hand. His appearance matched his name - dusty red hair and a dusting of blotchy freckles.

"Good to meet you, too, Dustin."

He started his talk, "I'm afraid there's going to be a delay in the processing of the church's insurance claim."

"I don't understand. We pay our premiums in a timely manner."

"Yes, Mrs. Jackson, you're correct. Unfortunately, the last several cases of church copper theft in this area turned out to be inside jobs. We need to conduct an investigation in conjunction with the local police department to be sure this claim is genuine."

So, they thought one of us stole it. Ain't that somethin! Pay all this money all these years, and the minute you want some of it back, they got to make sure *you* ain't the crook.

"How long will it take to conduct the investigation?" *Bet not take us into the heat of July.*

"Roughly ten business days, Mrs. Jackson. Depends on the communication between our office and law enforcement."

I certainly wanted to give Mr. Dustin Colbert a piece of my mind, but I knew better. This man had a job to do at work and probably mouths to feed at home. I reckon his boss probably had done told him they was losin' too much money behind these copper thieves; had to slow down what's going out 'till they could get more to come in.

Well, wasn't no use in me getting all riled up and actin' all ugly on behalf of Mt. Zion and Jesus Christ Himself. Couldn't have Dustin going home and telling his wife the worst meeting he had that day was with the people of God.

"Dustin, Angela or me will be calling you to check the status of our claim on a regular basis. Right?" I nodded at her, she nodded back. No harm in letting him know we meant business.

"I welcome your calls," he said, standing and pulling out two business cards. He gave one to me and one to Angela.

"Thank you, Dustin. Angela will talk to you tomorrow."

"Yes, ma'am."

We walked him to the door and let him out. As soon as he backed out my driveway, I had a few words with Angela in the kitchen. "You call him every day so he can be sure and keep our folder on top of his stack."

"Yes, ma'am."

"And, sweetie, why didn't you call Rev. Martin so he could be in on this meeting?"

She shook her head, shrugged her shoulders. "I don't know. I really didn't think I needed him here."

These young girls got to learn, but I guess it ain't their fault if nobody ever showed 'em what all a man is good for. "I know you smart and you perfectly capable of handling business. But don't underestimate the power of a man looking another man in the eyeballs when it come to stuff like insurance and used cars, hear?"

"Yes, ma'am," she said. "Mama B, since it looks like we can't meet at the church for a while, can you call the Mother's Board members and tell them to cancel until the building opens again? I'll get in touch with the other groups."

"Well..." I sighed. "I suppose the Mothers can meet here. Matter fact, all the women's groups can meet here 'til the church gets fixed. Maybe one of the brothers will open up a home for the men to meet. No need in stoppin' everything on account of the enemy's work. Can't give him what he wants."

"You're right, Mama B. Thank you. You are so helpful."

I caught a little twitch in her voice. "What's the matter?"

"Seems like since I became the church secretary, we've had all these issues. You think maybe I'm a jinx?"

"First of all, *these* ain't issues. When the church had a skunk family in the attic, *that* was an issue. Second, honey, you a child of God. Jesus lives in you, you live in Him, can't be no jinx in you."

We caught hands and prayed, asking God to oversee the claim, help the church get situated in the meanwhile and, most important, give Angela a clearer revelation of who she is in Christ. How much He love her, what all He done for her on the cross.

She left the house and I went back in the kitchen for my study. Added her name to my prayer list. *Jinx my foot! I wish a jinx* would *come up in my house. Be a whole bunch of ugly!* Made me mad just thinking about how the enemy done deceived her with all this jinx foolishness. Also made me think maybe she's dabbling in some stuff she ain't got no business. Horoscope, tarot, palm readin', or listening to a bunch of superstition, God forbid.

Soon as I finished my quiet time, here come Cameron's little feet shuffling into the kitchen. Rubbing his eyes, stretching. "Morning, Mama B."

"Morning, Cameron."

Though he and I hadn't spent much time together at all, he came right over and hugged my neck like we'd been doing this every day of his life. And I hugged him back just the same. He scooted right up next to me, looked down at the papers, pens, and books I had spread out across the table.

"Whatchu reading?"

"Oh, the Bible and a little book about patience."

He yawned. "You writing too?"

"Yes. I keeps a journal."

"Whatchu write in there?"

I tilted my head to one side. "Sometimes I write stuff I want to remember from the Bible or a book. I write stuff to God, and I write down what He tells me back."

Cameron's eyes got big as saucers. "God talks to you?"

"All the time."

"What does He say?"

"Well, He answers questions. Prayers. Tells me what to do. What not to do. Who needs help. Such and thus."

Then his eyes squinched up, suspicious-like. "Mama B, are you telling me the truth?"

Lord knows *my* BigMomma would have knocked the fire out of me for questioning her, but I got no problem answering kids so long as they ain't disrespectful. "What make you think I'm not tellin' the truth?"

He leaned over my arm, cupped his mouth and whispered into my ear, "'Cause I already know about Santa Claus."

"Aaaah." I sat back, winked at him. "Well, trust me on this one, Cameron. Santa Claus ain't even in the same category as God."

A little bitty dimple showed up in his smile, made my heart all warm inside.

Son was missing out.

Cameron switched to his favorite subject. "Whatchu got to eat?"

"Let's see. We could make oatmeal."

"Okay." He hopped up from the table and followed me to the cabinets.

"Bend down there and get me a big pot."

Before I knew it, Cameron was sprawled out on the floor, reaching all the way back for my good, slow-cooking pot. *This child coming in handy already.*

Cameron loaded his hot cereal with almonds and cranberries. Said he'd never seen brown sugar before, but he wanted to try it. We had almost finished eating before Nikki got out of bed and made her way in.

"Morning," she mumbled, pulling her robe closed.

"Hey, Nikki-Nik. You want something to eat? We got a little oatmeal left."

"Nosiree. I don't eat breakfast. I'm trying to lose this weight." She patted her behind twice. She hovered over Cameron a second, then bent down to kiss his forehead.

"Nikki, the last thing you need if you tryin' to lose weight is a empty stomach. Sit down here and let me make you some oatmeal. Fiber keep you full all day."

Nikki laughed and plopped herself in a chair. "If anybody knows how to keep it together, it's you, Mama B. Still got your shape, your smooth, even brown skin. Your hair is gray, but it's that pretty, shiny gray. You live on your own with no help. What gives? And how do you stay so small?"

"God's been gracious to me. But I don't know if I'd call a hundred and sixty-five pounds small, seeing as I'm only five seven." I stirred a little water and a pat of butter into the last of the oatmeal and turned on the fire.

"Mama B, I haven't weighed a hundred and sixty-five pounds since I was in junior high."

I turned from the counter and faced her. "Chile, how tall are you?"

"Five six."

"And how much you weighin'?"

"Two-ten, two-twenty."

"Ooh, yes, that's too dadgum big." *Lord, forgive me.* Had to reel my face back to the neutral zone and try to keep from making her feel bad.

"Well, you sure doing a good job of hiding it. And you cute as a button, Nikki-Nik."

She laughed again and put her chin in between her plump palms. Looked up at me with those brown eyes like I was her long, lost momma. "You know you're the only person who can talk to me like this. Go ahead, though. Tell me the secret to looking like a model all my life."

I told her, "I haven't always shopped in the regular section of the store. Had those four kids, packed on the pounds in my thirties and forties.

"But when I hit fifty and my friends started going down with heart attacks and strokes and going to dialysis three times a week. I took my big behind to that group weight loss program over at the First Baptist. Thank God He let me live long enough to change my habits 'cause, honey, I done seen the end of a lifetime of wild eatin' and I tell you one thing, it surely ain't pretty.

"Anyway, that's my secret."

"*What's* your secret?"

"Eat right and exercise."

She smacked her lips. "That's no secret, Mama B."

"Folks act like it is. But then again, folk act like reapin' the benefits of livin' by the Book is a big surprise, too."

Chapter 5

Soon as I got off the phone catching up with Debra Kay — she the only child I really need to talk to if I want to know what's going on with all my kids — I heard Libby Maxwell's car pulling up in the driveway. Got myself up from the table and joined her outside.

One thing about Libby: she was always on time or early. Made sense, though. She didn't have CP time, seeing as she wasn't colored. She went by whatever it say on the clock.

That was one of the first things I didn't like about Libby. And she said she didn't like how I come draggin' into the weight loss meeting right at the stroke of ten, but she overlooked me and I overlooked her. We ended up making friends with each other while we was shrinkin' down to a healthy size.

That was over twenty years ago. We'd been walking Monday, Wednesday, and Friday mornings ever since, weather permittin'.

Libby wore a pink jogging suit and white tennis shoes. We almost matched except my shirt had a little blue on the sleeves.

"Hey, Libby."

"Mornin', B."

She motioned toward Nikki's green Chevy truck. "Look like you got company."

"My granddaughter and her son."

"Nikki? The one we prayed about last week?"

"In the flesh," I laughed.

She took off walking, swinging her arms, I joined right in step.

"How long she stayin'?"

"Can't rightly say. We haven't had the talk yet. Right now I'm trying to see where she is in her head. Said she's coming from a bad situation."

Felt my heart rate increasing and I stretched my stride a little wider. Libby got us up to doing a mile in twenty minutes. We walk from my house to hers and back, or vice versa when I drive over to her house every other time. Two miles altogether.

"Well, at least you finally get to see her. You talked to Son?"

"Not yet. He might not be too happy about her being here. You know he thinks everybody always out to take advantage of me."

"Guess we better pray the Lord work on his heart next."

She asked about Geneva Phillips.

"They still got her up in that fancy cancer place in Oklahoma. Rev. Martin don't know much."

"Well, sometimes no news is good news."

We got to talking about Libby's family, too. Her baby girl, Macie, just finished her Master's degree in nursing. Jeremiah, her grandson, hurt his leg real bad playing soccer. Said they'd probably have to put a pin through his bone.

"Bad thing is, he's only thirteen. Need the Lord to heal him in a way that won't stop him from growing right," she said.

"Amen and amen."

By the time we got to the middle of our walk, we were both a-huffin' and a-puffin'. We made a pit stop for a drink of water at Libby's house. Her husband,

Peter, come in with the Dallas Morning News in one hand, a cane in the other.

"Morning, B."

"Right back atcha, Peter. Any good news in the paper?"

He hugged me and shook his head. "Now, B, you know better than that. Way better than that."

Libby grabbed the paper from him. She didn't like to see him without a free hand since he took a fall the year previous. Libby always did her best to make sure Peter got everything he need. Always making a fuss over him, and he let her. That's how it was with me and Albert, too.

"How are things at the Mt. Zion?"

I didn't want to advertise the enemy's work, but since Peter asked, I told him the truth—starting with the good news first. "Well, we got an insurance policy, so everything's gonna be fine. But somebody stole the copper out the air conditioning system."

He straightened up a bit. "Don't say?"

"Sure did. They gon' fix it in a little while, though. We just got to figure out a way to have our meetings and whatnot 'til they get it together."

"B, you know the doors of First Baptist always open if y'all need the building for somethin'," he offered kindly. Nice to have a friend whose husband is a pastor.

I shouldn't have been surprised by Peter's suggestion. That's one thing about Peter and Libby: they would give away the last cup of milk in their icebox to help somebody.

"Well, Peter, we may have to take you up on that offer if they don't get it fixed soon."

"Y'all welcome to join us in service or hold your own service soon as we get out. You give Libby the word, the church is open. Full way open"

"Thank you, Peter. Sure do appreciate the offer."

He waved his hand and shuffled on over to the fruit basket. "Ain't no problem, B. No problem at all."

Libby took my empty glass, rinsed it in the sink, and put it in the dishwasher alongside hers. "Shame all this crime moving into Peasner."

Peter commented, "That's the price of progress, Libby. Price of progress."

Me and Libby got back to our exercise, heading to my house. Sun a little higher in the sky by then. "We better start a lil' earlier Wednesday." I suggested.

"Yeah. Summertime setting in on us."

Kathy Woodridge come outside and waved at us. "I'm gon' join y'all one of these days."

"Kathy, you been sayin' that for years," Libby laughed, waving back.

"I don't know. But I sure wish the mailman give y'all my mail 'cause y'all more regular than he is."

Libby put her hand on my shoulder and we like ta almost lost our pace laughing with Kathy.

Chapter 6

By Wednesday morning , it was clear I had to get my words together so I could have the talk with Nikki. Get to the bottom of why she was in Peasner and why she wasn't goin' to work every day. I thought maybe her and Cameron needed a place to stay while she saved up enough money to put down on a new apartment. But the way she was goin, I didn't see no move-out in sight.

Well, let me tell the whole truth. I was getting antsy. Cameron was good for bending down and even lifting up couches so I could vacuum, but he was an eating machine. When he wasn't chomping down on a sandwich, he was playing shooting-type video games. Maybe that's what I really didn't like. My kids used to play outside with each other and with their friends until the lights came on. Had to call 'em inside. Wasn't any kids on our street for Cameron to play with just yet. They probably wouldn't be there until later in the summer when their parents needed a break. But I couldn't take him setting his rump in that chair between every meal. It ain't natural for a child to sit up in front of a screen all day, I don't care what nobody say.

I had to start finding other ways to put him to work.

Nikki was another one with a blue glow on her face all the time. On her cell phone texting all day.

Now, I liked technology – had me an email box, myself, on my iPhone. Check it every now and then. I even know how to do those text messages. But you can't keep you face in front of those doo-dads all the time. Mark my words – it's gon' be just like cigarettes and lead paint. Fifty years after they done got everybody exposed to it, they gon' come out with a study sayin' all these computers and phones is bad for your health – messin' up folks' eyes, throwin' off the babies' attention span. Hmph. I ain't gon' wait for the government to tell me what common sense already have.

Anyhow, I had to have a meeting with Nikki 'bout her plans, once she finally got up. "Morning Nikki-Nik. What you up to today?"

"Nothing much."

"Well, I was wondering about that. You on vacation?"

She opened both sides of my icebox—refrigerator and freezer—and stood there searching. Look like about five dollars worth of energy come flying out in all the frost. *Lord, I don't even want to see my light bill at the end of the month.*

"I guess you could say I'm on vacation."

"You laid off? Between jobs? Fired?"

She sighed, slumped her shoulders. "Fired."

"What happened?"

With her backside still to me, she explained, "I broke up with my boyfriend, J.T., and was promptly fired from my job as a receptionist at the transmission shop he and his cousin own."

"Hmph. Businesses and beaus don't mix. Happen every time."

"Tell me about it. But it's probably a good thing I left there anyway. I think they're laundering money."

She tucked the carton of orange juice under her arm, grabbed the jug of milk, and pulled down a box of cereal from the top of the refrigerator. "What kind of cereal is this?"

"All natural. Rolled oats, nuts, dried fruits."

"Do you have *anything* unhealthy to eat first thing in the morning?"

I pushed my morning study materials aside. "I try not to. But if you must, I got some Bisquick in the pantry. Syrup. You can make yourself some pancakes."

"Cameron already ate?"

"Yes. I sent him outside to pull up any weeds he could find. Told him I'd give him a few dollars."

Nikki shook her head. "I'm sure he ran outside when you told him he could earn some money."

I chuckled. "He sure did." I stood up and looked out the back window with Nikki. Cameron had collected a small pile of weeds, but he must have abandoned that effort for a pretend swordfight. He was jumping, kicking, swinging a tree branch. Now that's what I like to see. Kids breathing fresh air and using their imagination.

"He's a good boy, Nikki. You're doing a good job."

"Thank you."

"Where's his daddy these days?"

Nikki stepped away from the window. Got all busy with her cereal again. "Cameron's father is locked up. He's got a pretty long sentence."

Lord, bless his mother's heart. "Hmm. What for?"

"Trying to make quick money."

I wondered if he was the drug-sellin' type or the copper-stealin' kind. "You think he'll be a decent influence on Cameron when he gets out? Sometimes a man makes a bad choice in a bad circumstance. Don't necessarily mean he'll do it again."

"I appreciate you trying to see the bright side of things, but nobody in Cameron's family is a good influence. They're all a bunch of ghetto-fabulous losers." She gathered her cup and bowl, scooted my Bible and pens over a little, and took a seat at the table. "Cameron's only got me."

Hmph. She talked about Cameron's daddy like he's the only one in the wrong. I mean, sometimes you got to wonder who's got the biggest problem: the fool or the one who fell for him?

"No sense in talking about him so bad. You know anybody else who can help Cameron learn how to be a man?"

She shook her head.

I sat across from her. "Think you ought to give your daddy a call?"

She stuffed her mouth with a spoonful of cereal. All of a sudden, her face get all bunched up. She took a big swallow. "Mama B, this cereal tastes like pieces of cardboard."

"Just 'cause it ain't smothered in sugar don't mean it's nasty. Give yourself a few days to re-train your taste buds, it'll be all right after while."

She shook her head and took another scoop. Must have been hungry because she kept on eating.

"So, what you think about calling Son?"

"Mama B, my daddy's wasn't there for me. What makes you think he's gonna be there for my son?"

I breathed hard, trying to think about how to have this talk with Nikki without bringing up all the past. Lord knows my son and her mother started this whole bunch of mess. Shoot, makes me wonder where Albert and I went wrong with him.

Chapter 7

I could tell by the way she avoided my eyes, she really didn't want to talk about her Daddy. But she needed to think about her son. Since she picked a questionable father for Cameron, she ought to at least be willing to find a good substitute.

"Your daddy is older now. Got more sense than he did back when you were born. Plus, he never had a boy. This may be his only chance to do all the things men do with younger menfolk in a family. Go fishing, hunting. Stuff he didn't do with his daughters, he can do with Cameron. "

She dropped her spoon in the bowl. "And what about Miss Wanda?"

I rubbed my hand on Nikki's arm. "You let me handle Wanda. She listens to me. And she's got more sense, now, too. I reckon your momma does as well. People do grow up and mature after while. Most of 'em, anyway."

Nikky shook her head. "All I know is, Cameron and I have been getting along fine without his father or my father in our lives. You're the only one in the whole Jackson family I deal with, and that's fine by me. If I never talk to my father again, I'm good."

"Cameron never asks about his grandparents?" I asked her.

She nodded. "He does, sometimes. And I remind him that he has grandparents. My mom and you. When you send him gifts at Christmas and his birthday, he knows he has family."

"He also has aunts and uncles," I added. "And cousins."

She rested her spoon on the rim of the bowl. "I don't mean to be rude, but you seem to have forgotten that I am the product of an affair. My father, his wife, and my mother—the other woman—have never gotten along and they never will. I'd rather live my life without my father than be treated like a red-headed stepchild every time I'm around him and the rest of my so-called family."

There, she'd done it. Thrown it all out on the table like a big, black blob. Ugly, sticky. I gave another sigh.

"I'm sorry if I hurt your feelings," she quickly apologized, resuming her meal. She swallowed again. "The rest of them are so distant. You're the real thing, Mama B. No matter what was going on between my daddy and my momma, you still kept in touch with me all these years. That's why I knew Cameron and I could come here." It was her turn to rub my arm now.

Good Lord, I had almost forgotten the whole point of my conversation. Had to wind it down and switch channels. "Baby, I could never forget about you. You my blood, you mine no matter what happened with my son and the faults he had when he was your age. I'm always here for you.

"But now we got to talk about your plan for gettin' back on your feet. You need some help gettin' a job?"

She put a hand over her mouth to keep the cereal from spilling out while she laughed.

I raised an eyebrow 'cause I didn't see nothing funny.

"How you go from telling me how much you love me and you're always here for me straight to I-gotta-get-out-of-here?"

"It's *because* I love you that you can't stay here forever. I gives help, not handouts. So, let's start at the beginning. What you runnin' from? Got to be more than just a boyfriend."

Once she regained her composure, she answered, "J.T." She inhaled and exhaled again. "OK, here it is. I broke up with him because he started hitting me. Then, like I told you, he and his cousin fired me. I thought that was the worst he could do. But then he started stalking me—following me to job interviews, leaving notes on my car window. He walked Cameron home from school one day. Then when I opened the door to let Cameron in, J.T. rushed inside my apartment and started an argument.

"He's crazy, Mama B. I needed to put some space between me and him for a while, so I broke my lease and left."

Even though she'd told me a little more, I got the feeling she still hadn't told me everything. Maybe that's all she could come to grips with for now. "I sure want you to be prayerful."

"Oh, don't worry. I've got a little money in savings, and my car is paid for, so I'm good for now. I plan to give you something on bills and groceries. I just need a break, you know? Raising Cameron is a lot of work."

Skin rolled in between her eyebrows and I knew exactly what she meant. When Albert took vacation from work once a year, I would take my vacation, too, and stick him with the kids for at least two or three days just so I could go somewhere and put my feet up.

Every mother needs to catch her breath every now and then. "Yeah, Nikki-Nik, I do understand. And I'm glad to help you rest on a few laps of the rat race. But I don't think it'll hurt to get a plan goin' for when you get back in it. That's all I'm saying."

She shrugged. "I hear you. I'll start looking first thing Monday morning. Give J.T. time to find another girl and get his mind off me before I head back into the city looking for a job."

"Sounds like a plan. And in the meanwhile, I'd like you to get up and get some clothes on and come to the food pantry with me today. Help serve lunch to some people less fortunate than you, some of 'em ain't got nobody at all to turn to."

Cameron come bounding through the door, sweat dripping down his face. "Mama B, it's a snake out there!"

"What it look like?"

"Green and skinny. He about this long." The short width between his hands showed me the snake was pretty small.

"That's just a grass snake. No harm."

"Can I catch it?"

Nikki yelled "no" at the same time I said "yes." She and I looked at each other.

"A snake?" she squealed.

"That's what boys do," I filled her in.

She shivered. "Eew!"

I turned back to Cameron. "Your grandfather and your great Uncle Otha used to catch grass snakes all the time. Lady next door got a little pond in her back yard, sometimes the snakes wiggle over to our yard."

"Who's uncle Otha?" Cameron wanted to know.

Shame he didn't know his own people. "Otha is my other son.

"Go 'head and get a mason jar out the cabinet. See if you can't trap the snake in there. Be careful with it, and be gentle."

"What's a mason jar?" he asked next.

Nikki laughed. "I'll get it for you."

That girl made me proud. I only wished I could have gotten her in my house one week every summer like I did with the other grands. She might not be a single mother if I'd had the chance to speak into her life. But her Momma kept her at a distance. Can't say I blame her, though. She thought Son was going to leave Wanda, but Son got a clue before the divorce from Wanda was finalized and decided to try and save his family.

Poor Nikki got the short end of the stick. But I had a mind to sow whatever good I could into her for whatever bit of time God saw fit to let her and Cameron stay with me.

I sent Son a text message later on that night. Told him his daughter and grandson was at my house for a spell.

He sent me one letter back: **K.**

Chapter 8

Friday evening, the Titus 2 wives' ministry class convened at my house. The leaders, Janice Jamerson and LaTonya Wilcox, got to my house a quarter 'til seven to get prepared. They supposed to been giving the women a cooking lesson that particular night.

Sure was glad to see this ministry carrying on. Ophelia and I started it about fifteen years before, when both our husbands was still alive. But since they deceased, we let it pass on to the next generation 'cause it's kind of hard to talk to women about problems we ain't never gonna face no more.

Plus, me and Ophelia wasn't as encouragin' about husbands no more. Used to be we thought if you prayed and cried enough, God would change your husband. It happens sometimes, but we got no such exact promise from Him in the word, and you can't stand on what God didn't promise.

Not sayin' wives ought to give up on their husbands or their marriages, just sayin': might be God's will for you to practice your love walk, learn to keep your joy and peace no matter what while you married in this life, then y'all part ways at the pearly gates. He go his way and you go your way with Jesus.

Well, that ain't what the wives want to hear, so Ophelia and I did the right thing by turning it over to Janice and LaTonya. They could keep hope alive better.

Those two come in with pots and pans and five bags full of groceries plus soda pop, ice and paper plates.

I kissed them both on their cheeks as they trailed through the doorway.

"Mama B, you look so nice. Got your little capris and cheetah print top," LaTonya complimented me.

Janice added, "Please. She always looks good. Wait a minute. Let me see your glasses." She put her face all in mine, then hollered out, "Girl, she got cheetah print on the side of her glasses, too."

"Go on, Mama B. I ain't mad atcha," LaTonya laughed.

I waved them off. "Y'all come on in here."

"How many people y'all expect?" Much food as they had, must have been half the church. Then again, everybody know Janice and LaTonya could cook. They cakes and pies be the first to sell out at the fall festival.

"Ten or fifteen," LaTonya said, "but they always want to take a little home to their families so we got a lot more."

"Thank you so much for opening up your home to us," Janice said. "We could have had the class at my house, but since everybody already knows where the church is, it's just easier to have the meeting here."

"No problem. I'm glad to have y'all. What you cooking tonight?"

"My own special recipe chicken enchilada casserole," Janice beamed.

"With turtle brownies," LaTonya added.

"Sounds good. How can I help?"

"Mama B, you sure you want to get your clothes all dirtied up?"

"Got my apron right here."

We got busy washing chicken, dicing onions and tomatoes, grating cheese. Those gals turned my kitchen into one of those TV shows – had everything ready to pour and mix by the time the rest of the wives got there.

Nikki joined us for the meeting while Cameron sat in the front parlor reading a book I had made...well, *encouraged* him to get when I took him to the library after me and Libby finished our walk. Had to do something to get him out from in front of the tube. Thank God, the librarian knew exactly what books an 8-year-old boy would want to read. We checked out five that didn't have all the witchcraft. We brought the books home, and Cameron had been reading a good two hours with no end in sight.

Around seven-thirty, all the ladies moved into the kitchen to start the lesson. Nikki gave everybody the sheet of paper with the recipes on the front and back, and we all started watching and taking notes. I told them to help theyself to anything they wanted.

LaTonya started off with the dessert since it would take the longest to cook. She got the batter going, then remembered they forgot the butter. She saw my low-calorie margarine in the icebox and shook her head. "Mama B, where's your *real* butter?"

"Honey, I ain't had real butter in this house since my husband went on to be with the Lord."

Chile, they all looked at me like I'm crazy. So quiet you could have heard an ant tinkle on a cotton ball!

"Well, what *do* you use for butter?" Janice asked with question marks all over her face.

I got up from my chair and walked toward the fridge. "You can use applesauce instead of butter. Less calories. Better for you. Still tastes good."

Everybody in the room said "Oooh" and "I didn't know that."

Sister Williams's daughter asked. "My husband just got diagnosed with diabetes, we definitely need to cut back on the calories. What do you substitute for cheese?"

"Ain't no substitute for cheese. But if you get the right brand, you can get the two-percent kind. It melts just as good."

She smacked her lips. "My husband is *not* going to eat low-fat cheese."

I wagged my pointer finger back and forth twice. "Honey, you don't *tell* him it's low-fat. You just cook it and he'll eat it. I switched my family from ground beef to ground turkey real gradual-like. They didn't even know what hit 'em."

Now they all had their eyes on me, but I didn't want to steal the show and make 'em feel bad about eating all this enchilada stuff. I sure wasn't gone feel bad when I fixed my plate. No harm in eating wild every once in a while. Just can't make it a lifestyle.

"Let's go ahead and finish with the meal, and I'll give y'all some more ideas later."

"Yes ma'am."

Inside my heart, I felt real good, too, 'cause I like helping peoples, and I like to see the young women take care of their families. God fixed it to where can't nobody else on earth completely satisfy a man like his wife.

His ways so smart.

Chapter 9

Reverend Martin called an emergency meeting for church leaders Saturday, but I couldn't make it on account of I spent most of the day in Dallas shopping with Nikki and Cameron for church clothes.

They could have came on to church in what they had packed. Church ain't about the clothes you wear. But my great grandson ain't had no kind of dress shoes, no belt, nothing to wear in case of a funeral or to give a speech at the schoolhouse. And I don't know what kind of job Nikki think she gon' get with all those tights and oversized shirts she had done hung up in the closet.

I believe every male ought to have one good black suit with a tie, and every female ought to have one black dress she can wear year-round. Period. Can't tell you how many times I done bought a suit or a dress for somebody so they could pay last respects looking respectable.

Anyhow, the three of us squeezed into my little MINI Cooper and rode over to the closest mall.

I got Reverend Martin's text message while we was out shopping. Had to call Henrietta (she don't do no texts) and ask her to sit in the meeting at the coffee shop on behalf of the Mother's Board. About two hours later, after I got all the stuff for Nikki and Cameron, I was in the dressing room of *Chico's* trying on a few things for myself when Henrietta called me back just a-cryin' and a-sniffin'.

"B, Pastor Phillips done took a leave of absent."

My chest started thumping real hard. "What happened?"

"Well, he said the cancer hospital in Oklahoma gon' release Geneva. Said there's nothing else they can do for her. Sending her back to Texas. She 'bout to go any minute now. Got more tubes coming out of her than anybody ever seen. Pastor want to be by her side every minute she got left."

"Oh no," slid out of me.

"Yes. This is awful, just awful," she sobbed.

I was close to crying myself until the Holy Spirit told me to stop and consider the messenger. Henrietta hadn't bit more seen Geneva lately than me. How would she know Geneva got a bunch of tubes comin' outta her? And why would they send Geneva on a long trip back to Texas if she was in that critical of condition?

What Henrietta said wasn't addin' up. Not tryin' to talk bad about my church member, but she did have a habit of overexaggeratin'. I'd have to wait until I saw Reverend Martin at church to get the complete record of what was actually said.

"Well, let's pray for Geneva and Pastor right now," I prompted. Then we both went before the throne and thanked God for His peace, His healing, and everything Jesus already did for us on the cross. We prayed for Pastor's well-being and for Geneva's health. "Amen."

Henrietta said, "Amen," and kept right on going. "That ain't all, B."

Now why she couldn't tell me everything before we prayed? "What else?"

"Reverend Martin done got us a enter- in pastor."

I mashed the phone to my ear. "A what?"

"Enter in. He gon' *enter in* while Pastor Phillips is gone. Be our regular preacher for the time being."

She meant *interim*, but I wasn't gon' embarrass her with the correction. Plus, I know my English ain't always perfect, either. Pots got no business callin' kettles black.

"Will the other pastor start tomorrow?"

"Yes. It's somebody the deacons brought in a few times before. Jerome or Janeem? Jamaal?"

I said, "Jamaal Dukes?"

"Yeah, that's his name."

Someone in Reverend Martin's extended family, I knew. Last time Rev. Dukes came to the church and preached for the church anniversary, he preached like he come from one of those churches with all that hootin' and hollerin' and carryin' on, but barely crack open the Bible.

That was a while back, though. Like I said before, sometimes it take a while for a preacher to come into his own behind the pulpit, and it don't help the process none with people like me in the audience lookin' at him like he Daffy Duck.

"Well, let's pray for him, too, that the Lord use him well, that we can give him a good congregation to practice more preaching, and that his presence will be a relief to Pastor."

Henrietta snapped, "Nuh uh. I ain't prayin' for him. I'm prayin' *against* him. I'm too old to have somebody practicin' on me. Too many things goin' wrong with me right now. And Pastor Martin done already signed Jamar up without even askin' anybody!"

Lord knows, I tried to calm Henrietta down. "Pastor Martin represents the Deacons, Ssister. I'm sure they all agreed before he ever set up the meeting with the rest of the leaders."

"Well, I don't. I don't like Jerome nor his wife. She too uppity. Always got on a bunch of flashy jewelry and perfume, fancy clothes."

I looked at myself in the mirror. Henrietta probably would say the same thing about the gold jacket and black sequin tank top I was sho nuff 'bout to buy and wear to church the next day. "Now you know we can't judge people by what they—"

"I'm not just talkin' bout what him and his wife wear," she cut me off. "He can't preach! Just get up there and put the mic real close to his mouth so it sound like he got the Holy Ghost on him."

"Well, Henrietta, maybe he was raised in a Pentecostal church. You know that's how they do. No harm, it's just a different—"

"I don't care if he from a penny-cost or no-cost! Last time he came, my ears was ringin' the rest of the day. I ain't finna sit up here every week and get my eardrums blowed out, and I ain't movin' off the front row, either!"

Even though I half-way agreed with her about Jamaal, I could see we wasn't headed nowhere godly down this road of conversation. And I'd had enough of her not letting me finish my sentences.

"Don't get your pressure up, Henrietta. You got to remember he won't be here forever. Just until the Lord move on Geneva's health. I got to go now. I'll see you at church tomorrow. We still meetin' at First Baptist, right? Twelve-thirty?"

"Yes. Maybe you'll see me there, maybe you won't."

"Good-bye, Henrietta."

Chapter 10

Nikki got all dressed up in her sour face. Said she wasn't used to getting up and out on Sunday mornings.

"Mama B, we'll be the first ones there!"

"Exactly how I like it."

She whined some more. "Do we have to go to church every Sunday?"

"Chile, I don't leave nobody behind who's well and able to get up and go to church on the Lord's day. House rules."

Cameron wanted to know if he could take his book to church in case it got boring.

"No. The only book you read in church is the Bible." Part of me wanted to fuss at Nikki 'cause obviously this boy ain't gettin' trained right.

He frowned. "I don't have a Bible."

I patted him on his head. "We gon' have to fix that problem then, won't we?"

I suppose Libby and Peter had already gave Rev. Martin, Jamaal Dukes, and the choir a run of the building because everybody was in place and almost ready to start when I got there.

Libby and a few other ladies were combing through the padded green pews picking up trash people from their service had left behind and shoving the hymnals back in their slots. I come alongside her on the next row over and helped. Cameron helped, too, until we had walked down every one.

"Libby, this my great-grandson, Cameron."

"So nice to meet you! And how handsome you are! Spittin' image of Son."

"Ain't he though?" I agreed.

Cameron shook her hand properly. "Nice to meet you, too."

When she walked toward the trash can, Cameron looked up at me and asked, "Who's Son?"

Nikki had done took a spot on the very back row, so she couldn't hear us. Lord knows I wasn't tryin' to cause no mess, but the boy had a right to know his peoples. "Son's your grandfather."

"My friend at school, her name is Sierra. She calls her grandfather Paw-Paw. Can I call my grandfather Paw-Paw?"

"If he lets you, I suppose you could. Would you like to meet him?"

That boy's face lit up like somebody told him they was givin' out free donuts. "Yes! Yes! Yes!"

"I'll see about makin' that happen for you, Cameron. Keep that between me and you right now, you hear?"

"Yes, ma'am." He skipped on back to sit by his mother.

I overheard Peter telling Rev. Martin how to work the sound system. Then Libby joined them and told Rev. Martin that she and Peter were going home to have lunch. They'd be back later to lock up the church. She said some people from the men's fellowship team were meeting in the back of the church and could help us if we needed anything, then they left.

For some reason, Rev. Dukes still hadn't started the opening prayer by 12:45. Guess he was waitin' on more people to show up. He had conversations with Angela, talked to Clive on the organ, ran over and said something to his wife, called Rev. Martin over to the side. My goodness—who all he did he have to talk to?

Pastor Phillips 'bout worse than Libby when it comes to being exact on time for stuff. He start church right at whatever time he say, whether it's two people there or twenty. I guess Rev. Dukes starting a little later didn't hurt nobody, but it sure didn't set well with me.

In the meanwhile, I took another good look at First Baptist. Libby and Peter done a good job of keeping the church going. Nice, clean building. Bible studies on Wednesday night. Serving food to the community, helping pregnant teenage girls find couples to adopt babies. They sacrificed a lot to keep this ministry going.

First Baptist wasn't really all that much bigger than Mt. Zion. Just the ceilings were higher, tricked the eyes into thinking you were in a big old place when you wasn't.

Still waiting for somebody to get us going, I decided I might as well read a few scriptures and get my mind on the Lord. Just in time, too, 'cause Henrietta flopped her behind down right next to me, wearing her white usher uniform, even though she ain't served on that auxiliary in years.

She crossed her arms high on top of her bosom and rocked herself into a frenzy. "It's going on one o'clock! What he waitin' on?"

"I don't know."

Then Henrietta busted out singing, "Jesus getting us ready for that great day." She clapped and sung it a few more times before Clive picked her up on the organ. Guess he was ready to begin, too.

Finally, after Henrietta done ran through a whole medley of songs, about fifteen people—mostly women—come waltzing in the church and took the first three rows. None of them members of Mt. Zion.

Finally, Rev. Dukes got up to the podium and started singing along with the rest of us. He been waitin' on them the whole time, I saw.

Henrietta saw it too, 'cause she elbowed me all in my ribcage something awful. Leaned over and said, "Is he here for them or us?"

One of the guests took over the congregational number, sung herself happy and got their bunch to start the hollerin' early.

I just hoped we wasn't about to have a circus. Now, don't get me wrong: I believe in dancing, jumping, hollering, falling out, speaking in tongues, all that so long as the Spirit of God leads. I've done just about all of that myself, truth be told. My mother was a Baptist, but my father was born and bred Church of God in Christ. If he hadn't died when I was a little girl, I'm sure I would have COGIC all in my socks right now.

Got nothing against undignified praise.

What I do have a problem with is people just doin' stuff to be seen, be loud, tryin' to push your forehead down to the ground when they pray for you—that's what I got a problem with.

I used to think you couldn't discern what other people doin' cause they in the house of God, after all. But the Holy Spirit get grieved when folk mock Him. And since He alive in me, I can't help but get grieved, too.

Hmph. People be surprised how much He reveals once you get into the habit of listening to Him. I done had folks look me in the eye and tell me a lie, and the Holy Spirit whisper in me He lying, but don't say anything right now. Or I be listening to a preacher on the radio talk about something happened to him, and the Holy Spirit say That didn't really happen to him. He just made that up for the sermon.

Anyway, I saw already that me and Rev. Dukes wasn't on the same page, but I couldn't share none of my thoughts with Henrietta. Just add more fuel to her fire. I ignored her question about who Rev. Dukes was preaching for. Kept my eyes facing forward.

Lord, help my attitude and Henrietta's, too.

The choir sang, Deacon Bledsoe led the reading of the scriptures, Angela made the announcements, we took up an offering, and the next voice we heard was none other than Rev. Jamaal Dukes. (I think Rev. Martin knew we'd better get on with it.)

"Would you please turn with me to the book of Psalm. Chapter thirty-seven. Verse four."

Henrietta hunched me again. "He ain't gon' pray? Give honor to our pastor?"

"Henrietta, please."

She cut her eyes at me. Sat straight up, crossed her arms again.

Soon as I read the scripture, I had an idea where Rev. Dukes might be going. Of course, all the word is good for teaching—so long as you don't teach it out of context and twist it up like that snake Cameron was keeping in the jar.

"Church, I stopped by to talk to you today about two words. Dreams and desires."

"Amen," came from his cheerleading corner. "Preach it!"

"The scripture reads as follows. Delight thyself in the Lord, and he will give you the desires of your heart. Anybody in here got desires? Anybody in here got dreams?"

"Yes, sir," the congregation answered.

Thought I saw Henrietta nod.

"I know. Life's been hard on you. You been struggling to pay your house bills, your doctor bills, keep food on the table. I stopped by to tell you the struggle is over!"

"Yes!" came from the congregation.

"No more living from paycheck to paycheck. I'm telling you that car, that house, that job, that woman, that man—whatever you want from the Lord, you can have it!"

This time I saw Henrietta's hand go up, plain as day.

"All you got to do is give Him praise. Delight yourself—get happy about Him!"

"Yeah!" A few people jumped up.

"Holler for him like you hollerin' for the Cowboys!"

"Yeah!" came the reply again.

Then Henrietta shot up and waved a handkerchief at him. "That's my kinda preachin!"

I'm tellin' you, he put that microphone right up to his teeth and yelled, "I say holla!"

Good Lord, I hope Libby and Peter got some good speakers.

"Holla!" from even more people.

A lady from the other crowd scooted Clive off the organ. She played a dancin' tune for a good minute while everybody clappin' and hollerin'.

"Y'all sit down," Rev. Dukes said, running a cup towel over his bald head. "I'm going to preach this like it's my very last sermon because you never know when it might be. It is my determined will that in the time I have here at Mt. Zion Baptist church, however long or short, I make everyone as rich as they can possibly be. Is that alright?"

Henrietta calmed herself down and gave me a smirky smile. "Long as he gon' preach about gettin' more money, he might be alright with me."

I just put my head down in my Bible and wait for him to tell 'em the whole truth about this particular book of Psalm. Get to the next verse or even go back to the one before it.

But he never did.

Chapter 11

Soon as Rev. Martin gave the benediction, Nikki come running over to me cheesin' from ear to ear. "Mama B, I'm so glad you brought me to church. I can't wait to get rich! This is just what I needed to hear."

Rev. Dukes wife must have heard our conversation. She threw her nose up in the air, waltzed over, and stopped right between me and my granddaughter. "Hello, my sisters, my name is Cynthia Dukes. I'm Rev. Dukes's wife. So blessed to make your acquaintances."

"My name is Beatrice Jackson, but everybody calls me Mama B. This here is my granddaughter, Nikki." I looked around for Cameron, but he must have been outside with the other kids.

"We are so happy to be here," Cynthia said with a big smile on her face. Her peach lipstick matched the peach two-piece jacket and dress, but I could hardly see the rhinestone design for all the waves of hair flowing everywhere. Who these folk think they foolin' with all this fake hair?

Well, anyway, I guess that's how they do it these days. Maybe they ain't tryin' to fool nobody no more.

I figured Cynthia meant what she said about being glad to be at Mt. Zion. My question was *why* she was so happy to be at Mt. Zion.

Lord knows I don't like to think bad of people, but when something ain't right, it ain't right. Even if I can't quite put my finger all the way on it.

Nikki grabbed Cynthia's hand and give it a shake like the woman just offered her a job or something. "I soooo enjoyed the message today. Next week, when I start looking for my job, I am going to think bigger, beyond anything I've ever done because I know God wants nothing but the very best for me."

Angela joined our little crowd. "Mama B, you look so nice today."

"Mmm hmm. I was just admiring your blouse," Cynthia said.

"Thank you."

Angela said, "Cynthia, this is the lady I was telling you about. She's the one hosting the women's fellowships in her home, right behind the church."

Cynthia's brows slid up three inches. I didn't know what she had in mind, but I knew she wanted something.

"Mama B, my goodness, the Lord works in mysterious ways," she started in on me. "I was just telling Angela, I want to have the women's book club meeting at your house."

"Book club?"

Cynthia held my hands inside of hers, like we kids about to play a game of patty-cake. "Yes. The women from our home church have a strong book club. Discussing literature provides a wonderful opportunity for the women to fellowship and talk about real-life issues."

"Sounds great," Nikki chimed in.

Wasn't but a few days previous, I couldn't get my granddaughter to take a book off the shelf at the library!

Cynthia continued, "We also have a woman to woman group. We chit-chat and study the Bible from a woman's perspective. We'd love to meet this weekend with the ladies of Mt. Zion, if that's alright?"

I wasn't expectin' all that so quick-like. They just got here this morning and already trying to start new ministries.

"Ooh, I can't wait," Nikki bubbled over. "Can we do it, Mama B?"

Hearing my grandbaby excited about anything pertaining to church was music to my ears. "Well, I suppose it's not a problem, so long as Pastor Phillips agrees."

Cynthia clapped her hands. "Wonderful Jesus!"

She looked around and called, "Sister Karen! Sister Karen!"

A woman with just as much hair come down the center aisle so fast, look like she comin' to save a baby from a burning building.

"Yes, sister?"

"This is Mama B. Mama B, this is Karen. She's my armor bearer."

Karen had a genuine kindness in her warm eyes. I liked her already. Sometimes you can just tell when you come across good peoples, open hearts and eager to help. "Hello, woman of God."

"Hi, Karen."

"Karen, Mama B is going to host the woman to woman Bible study Saturday night. You two need to exchange numbers," Cynthia said—more like ordered—and walked away.

"Yes, ma'am." Karen got her cell phone out her purse in a hurry. "Mama B, may I have your number?"

"Certainly may. And I'll give you my email, too."

Nikki and I prepared a fruit tray along with Rotel dip and tortilla chips. I made the meat with half-turkey and half-ground beef.

I think Nikki was glad to be meeting with the ladies of the church. Her job-hunting wasn't going so good. She spent two days at the library looking stuff up on the internet, and she wore that same black dress to four or five places filling out applications. Still nobody called her back yet.

"Give it some time," I told her as I motioned for her to hand me a bowl so I could put the cheese squares in the microwave.

"I don't have much more left in my savings."

"Well, at least you had something to fall back on. You been smart about your money, I can tell. Lot of folks lose their jobs and be stuck out."

I wouldn't want to make her lazy by telling her, but she could stay with me long as she needed to, so long as I could see she was making an effort to get back on her feet. Got no problem helping people who's trying to help theyself.

"Thanks, Mama B. That's what I like about you." She had stopped cutting green peppers, put a hand on her hip, and looked at me.

"What?"

"Nobody had ever told me I was doing a good job with Cameron before you. All I've ever heard from my mother was how silly it was for me to get pregnant my senior year in high school and then *not* have an abortion. You make me feel like I made the best of the situation by giving birth to Cameron and doing everything I can to give him a good start in life."

"You got to know you made the right decision every time you look at him. He's something else, ain't he?"

The corners of her mouth turned up. "He sure is."

"What time Rev. Martin want the parents to pick up the kids from the movies?"

"Eight-thirty."

"Oh, good. We should be finished with the Bible study by then."

Somehow, Cynthia rounded up about ten female members of Mt. Zion between the ages of twenty-five and forty and got 'em all over to my house by six Saturday evening. Another seven women from wherever church they was from joined us. We had a full house. Had to run to the church and get some folding chairs out the fellowship hall.

Me and Nikki made sure every last one of them had a full bowl and a drink of pink lemonade. A couple of napkins. Showed them all where the bathroom was, and it was time to get going.

Karen opened up with a prayer, then Cynthia had everybody do an introduction.

When it came my time, I said, "My name is Beatrice, but everybody calls me Mama B. I love the Lord and now that my husband is gone on to glory, I'm married to Jesus."

They laughed a little. I know it sounds funny, but it sure is the truth.

Angela raised her hand. "Mama B, do you mind telling everybody how old you are?"

"Sure don't! I'm proud of my age. I'm seventy-two years old."

Everybody started gaspin' and hootin'. "No way!" "Nu uh." One of them asked me to pull out my license to prove it.

"You walk in the Lord's ways, He'll preserve you."

They tickled me. Way they was actin', you think I was Methusela. Seventy-two ain't all that old—it's just old to them 'cause they thirty and forty-something. But the older you get, the younger old people start lookin' to you.

After everybody finished telling if they married, how many kids they got, what kind of work they do, so on and so forth, Cynthia led everybody to the book of Isaiah, chapter nineteen, verse eleven. "If you are willing and obedient, you will eat the best from the land; but if you resist and rebel, you will be devoured by the sword. For the mouth of the Lord has spoken."

I was glad to hear her discuss something about loyalty to the Lord. I took a seat and rested from serving the women.

"Ladies, there are two conditions: be willing and obedient. You have to be willing to make a move. Willing to do what thus says the Lord. But beyond a willingness, you have to step out on faith in obedience. Amen?"

"Amen," from the room.

"You've heard that if you want something different, you have to do something different. I don't know about you, but I want what's here in the word. Eating the best and living beyond your wildest dreams, blessed in excess of what you can think or imagine. More money than you can count!"

"Amen." Louder now.

Here we go.

I looked over at Nikki and almost saw dollar signs dancing in her eyes. She was so hungry for work.

"And, ladies," Cynthia went on, "God has provided us a wonderful opportunity for such a time as this."

Karen got up, reached to the side of the couch and grabbed the handle of a super-size suitcase. I don't know how I missed them lugging that thing in, but they sure did sneak it past me.

Cynthia laid the luggage flat and unzipped it. She reached down and pulled out a black bodysuit-looking thing with a bunch of silver hooks up and down the front. Remind me of the old swimsuits men used to wear.

"Ladies," she stood up and announced real big and bold, "*this* is Body Enchantment."

What in the world?

"I've been selling these independently for three weeks, making serious money. This product sells itself because it makes women look up to three sizes smaller in less than fifteen minutes."

Mt. Zion women starts oooh-in' and aaah-in'. "I got to see this for myself."

Cynthia flipped her hair back. "Before I make the presentation to you about the business opportunity, you have to try it for yourself first."

"I'm ready," LaTonya hopped up.

I couldn't help myself. Raised my hand. Tried to make my voice sound real sweet. "I'm sorry…umm…I thought we was doin' a Bible study here tonight?"

Cynthia shook her head. "Mama B, there comes a time when you got to get up off your knees, close your Bible, and get to work. God's not going to give you the best of the land while you're sitting on your behind. You have to be obedient to Him! Give Him something to work with! Otherwise, you can't blame Him when you can't pay your bills." She took her eyes off of me. "Am I right?"

Everybody from her church gave her an amen.

Shantay Lewis, director of Sunday school since Geneva came down with the cancer, interrupted again. "Is this what you're going to discuss the rest of the night?"

"Well, yes, unless you've got something else on your mind, my sister," Cynthia replied, blinking quickly.

Shantay stood up, pulled her purse strap on her shoulder. "I've been to one of these parties before."

"Oh," Karen tried to stop her, "aren't you interested in the business opportunity?"

"No, thank you. You ladies have a good night."

Tell em, Shantay!

"Good Night," they all said with question marks in their voices.

Soon as Shantay shut the door behind her, Cynthia put her voice real low. "You can't make people believe."

Chile, I had to just get up and excuse myself 'cause I was 'bout to do like Jesus and turn over some tables, only I didn't want to scuff up my hardwood floors.

Chapter 12

First thing come to mind was I needed to call Ophelia, but Lord knows she would have come running straight up to my doorstep and bopped Cynthia upside the head with a large-print Bible.

I wanted to call Pastor Phillips, but I didn't want to worry him about this matter just yet. He got bigger problems, with Geneva and all.

Only One I should have rightfully called on, anyway, was the Lord. He got a dog in this fight.

While the ladies carried on, taking turns in the restroom trying on their Body Enchantment suits, I slipped off into my bedroom and rocked in my rocking chair. Closed my eyes and talked to the Lord.

Hoped Nikki could help them if they had any questions because, at the moment, I couldn't trust my mouth.

Lord, You and I both know this ain't right.

I was trying to get calmed down, but the more I thought about it, I knew I had to say something because we wasn't about to have no more surprise-pyramid-parties up in my house.

I didn't have high blood pressure but I sure felt my heart beatin' fast in my chest right then.

Figured I'd wait until we was down to the last few—hopefully just Cynthia and Karen—before I said something. Had to do it decent and in order, with as much love as I could scrape up. Maybe they didn't know any better. Maybe this just the way they do things at their church, nobody ever told them this whole set-up was a little off. Or a *lot* off.

Since I settled my mind with the thought that Cynthia and Karen wasn't trying to be disrespectful, just needed to be taught, I could stomach the whole thing a little better. Made my way back to the kitchen, looked in on the young ladies every once in a while so I wouldn't seem rude.

My tongue had all kind of bite-marks in it by the end of all these women squeezin' into those glorified girdles. That's all it was, really—except it cost almost two hundred dollars! Goodness, they could have had six months worth of group meetings at First Baptist, lost fifty pounds, *and* bought a new girdle for less than two hundred dollars!

Good thing Nikki didn't have much money left, 'cause I know she would have bought one. She starin' at Cynthia the whole night like that woman set the moon and the stars herself. Hard to blame Nikki, though. Cynthia was nice-lookin', well put together. All her verbs and words proper. She the kind of woman we had in mind for our daughters to be when we was marchin' for freedom and equality.

About eight o'clock, Karen started taking orders and signing people up for the pyramid. She was taking cash, swiping credit cards with a fancy doo-dad on her cell phone. Some of the ladies said they didn't have enough money—had to wait until the first of the month. Cynthia said she would take a post-dated check from a woman of God.

Most of them had cleared out by a quarter after. About that time, Nikki said she had to go get Cameron.

Good thing, too. I didn't want her to hear what I had to say to Cynthia and Karen. God always work stuff out so things don't have to be ugly.

The last woman, somebody named Alexis from their church, was the only one left to finish up her paperwork. From the way they talked, Cynthia must have been the highest on the pyramid. Then Karen, then Alexis. And under Alexis, people from Mt. Zion now.

They didn't have no closing prayer, not even ask the Lord to help them drive home safely. Nothing. Could have been a parent-teacher meeting, the way they ended.

I finished throwing all the napkins and empty cups away for the ones who forgot their manners. Probably got so caught up in looking like they lost weight, they didn't know how to act.

Karen and Cynthia were down on their knees, zipping up the suitcase, talking amongst themselves. I wasn't trying to overhear them, but I guess they was so busy they didn't realize I was in earshot.

"Ooh, girl," Cynthia drawled, "we must remember to bring air freshener next time."

Karen laughed a bit.

Cynthia edged it on, "Somebody forgot their deodorant. And, for real, I didn't think we would have one *big* enough for that sister in blue. She was huge! Almost broke my nails trying to stuff all that gut in!"

How you take folks money one minute and talk about 'em like dogs the next?

"Sister Cynthia, you know you need to stop talking about people like that," Karen said with a chuckle in her tone.

At least one of them had a little bit of sense.

Cynthia added, "It's the truth."

I know folks call that 'keepin' it real' nowadays. But it my day, we called it back-bitin'. I stepped into the den and spoke up before they could say anything else. "Y'all about packed up?"

"Praise the Lord, yes. And thank you again, Mama B, for letting us have the meeting here. It was such a great success. God's got a special blessing for you, woman of God." Cynthia said in a real strong tone; sound like she was up on her own pulpit.

"Well, Cynthia, I don't mind helping people. But, I need to talk to you about something. Sit down here a minute. You and Karen." I patted the cushion next to me on the love seat.

"Yes, ma'am," Karen obliged and sat beside me. Cynthia took the chair across from us.

"Now, I know you all have a business to run with this Body Enchantment. If this is what God has called you to do, I know He will put His hand on it and open all the doors you need to be successful. But you invited these people here on the premise of a Bible study meeting, and it wasn't."

Karen's eyes got real big. She looked to her leader for an answer.

"I fully comprehend what you're saying. But sometimes, we have to do what we have to do to reach the people of God and give them the knowledge they need. Particularly the people from the African-American community." Then Cynthia licked her lips, like she tryin' real hard to think of how she can explain herself in a way where I can understand her. "Maybe you've never heard this, but the Bible says God's people perish for the lack of knowledge in Hosea three and six."

No she didn't try to pull out the word on me! "And in the very next verse of Hosea, it says the people *rejected* knowledge, which is exactly what I'm trying to give you." I had done held it in long enough.

Her neck rolled back a little.

Didn't phase me none. "Now, I got no problem with the people of God having businesses and prosperin'. My husband and I were blessed beyond what most folks—black or white—in our time experienced. And I done hosted plenty Mary Kay and Amway and Tupperware parties here, trying to help people make money. Difference is, we *called* it what it was. And we sure didn't slap the Lord's name on it like some kind of endorsement, make people feel unholy if they didn't want to participate."

Karen still hadn't said a mumbling word. Sat there with her fingers laced across her belly.

Cynthia huffed a little bit. "We're only trying to enlighten and encourage the people of God. When the people make more money, the church makes more money to turn around and help others. That's what my husband and I are all about—empowering people. All I can do is apologize if you were offended by what we did."

I shook my head. "It's not me being offended I'm worried about. It's the Lord. Listen, if you want to have another Body Enchantment party here, you are more than welcome. But we 'gon call it a Body Enchantment party. And if you want to have a Bible study here, we can have that, too. But let's not mix up Body Enchantment with the word of God. That's all I'm saying.

Almost could see smoke comin' out of Cynthia's ears.

I couldn't worry about her being mad. We needed to get to an understanding. "Now is this book club meetin' y'all planning actually a book club meetin' or is it another recruitin' event?"

Karen ran intervention. "If you want us focus on the book, we can."

"That would be best."

I stood up so they could get the message this conversation was over. I had done heard them out, they had done heard me out, it was up to the Holy Spirit in both of us to show us the rest.

Plus it was going on nine o'clock and I don't entertain folks that late.

Chapter 13

For our second Sunday at First Baptist, Rev. Jamaal preached another one of his get-rich-quick sermons. This time, he didn't even bother to try and have a scripture to back it up. He put his hand on his chest and said, "This Sunday, I want to preach from my heart. Is that alright with y'all?"

Couldn't nobody beat Henrietta hollerin', "Go 'head, preacher!"

He continued, "I want to talk to you about what the Lord did for me and my wife. Give you some *real life* experience. Is that alright?"

Henrietta tilted her head toward me. "That's the best kind of preachin, you ask me."

"Not to me," I whispered back. "I need the word of God."

"Sometimes you need *more* than the word," she said. She pooched out her lips and turned her head back to the pulpit.

Far as I'm concerned, there's nothing more important than the love of God all wrapped up in His word and His Son. I couldn't take no more. For the first time in thirty-seven years, I tipped out of Sunday morning service early. Left Nikki and Cameron at church. Left my third Sunday homeless offering with Ophelia. Got in my car and drove the three miles from First Baptist back to my house. Slammed the door when I walked inside.

Lord, I'm sorry I left the church today.

First thing I did when I got home was get back in my prayer closet and ask the Lord to show me myself. I mean, got to be something wrong with me to get up and leave church early. And it can't be right for me to get so mad in my own Father's house.

I just love the Lord. And I can't stand to see nobody use Him for their own purposes. He's too good for folk to treat Him like He some kind of genie in a bottle, they just got to figure out how to rub Him the right way to get what they want.

But I can't be runnin' out the church every time something don't go my way, neither. If it wasn't Jamaal and Cynthia, the next pastor would probably do some things I didn't like, if Pastor Phillips didn't come back. Come to think of it, Pastor Phillips had did stuff I wasn't too keen on. I never walked out on his sermon, though.

Right or wrong, I couldn't deny the fact that people listened to Rev. Dukes. He had a gift for leadership. Only his second time preaching, and he got a few of Mt. Zion's deacons to stand on their feet, moanin' and leadin' him on—"Yes, sir!" "You tellin' the truth!"

I recognize anointing when I see it. Kinda reminded me of David, when he refused to kill Saul 'cause he knew Saul was chosen by God. Even though Saul wasn't actin' right.

Lord, I repent for being disrespectful to the preacher.

Since Rev. Dukes wasn't too interested in the word, I decided to turn on the television and catch one of my favorite ministers while my ground chicken burgers browned on the George Foreman grill.

Wouldn't you know, the Lord led me smack to a message about not arguing with people! Whoo, that's just like Him to teach me something even in my disobedience. Preacher had us in 2 Timothy, talking about a workman approved by God.

At first, I read it thinking about Rev. Jamaal and Cynthia and all their foolishness. But then I got down to verses twenty-three to twenty-five, where it talk about people getting into arguments with other folk.

I think that part was for me. Well, I know it was. Figured I probably shouldn't do ugly things like walk out of church right in the middle of the preacher's message. Made me look childish to the very people I called myself trying to help.

Nikki and Cameron got to be wonderin' why I made them go to church, then walked myself right out.

Well, wasn't nothing I could do about it by that point. I had done come out my shoes, and stockings and changed into my soft bra already. Too late to turn back now.

Cameron wasn't too crazy about salads, but he would eat a little lettuce and tomato if I put it on a burger with cheese. I knew he wouldn't be able to tell one way or another that he was eating chicken, not beef. Even Nikki ate just about anything I put in front of her so long as it didn't look overly healthy.

They both come through the door about an hour later than me. Service must have went long.

"Mama B, we home!" Nikki called out.

"I'm in the kitchen. Y'all get out of your Sunday clothes and come on in here and eat. Got burgers and baked beans."

Cameron rushed right in to see me instead. "Mama B, you alright?" He wrapped his arms around my waist, held on for dear life.

"Yes, I'm fine. Why you ask?"

"'Cause I saw you when you walked out the church. You looked like you were sick or something."

Out of the mouth of babes. I pushed him back, bent down to his eye level. "No, Cameron, Mama B wasn't sick. But I thank you for thinking 'bout me.

"Then why did you leave?"

"That's a good question, Cameron. It's not right to walk out of church—especially when the word of God is going forth."

Not that there *was* any word. Still. "I just had a bad thing going on, but I'm alright now. God met me here when I got home."

His mouth dropped open. "God was here?"

"Yes, Cameron, God is everywhere."

"Oh. That's good 'cause there's a lot of broke people who need God to come to their house and give them some money."

"Is that so?"

"Yes ma'am. Pastor Drake said everybody in the church is going to be a millionaire. Then all the people start shoutin', like this."

He jumped up out of his chair, threw his hands up in the air, and started dancing a holy dance before I had a chance to stop him. "Haba-laba-laba! Shamazzakamala! Thank you, Jesus!"

I slapped my stirring spoon against the pot. "Cameron, stop that!"

He froze. "Yes, ma'am."

"Go put on your play clothes."

"Yes, ma'am."
Help me, Lord.

Chapter 14

I couldn't hardly eat after talking to Cameron. Sat there picking over my food, then finally just went on and gave him the second half of my chicken burger.

Later on, I called Ophelia. "You think we can get the mother's board together this week? We need to pray."

She almost whispered to me, "You been thinkin' what I'm thinkin' about Rev. Dukes?"

Had to answer, "I'm thinking we need to meet with the deacons, and pretty soon. My great-grandson thinks God is a Sugar Daddy."

She tisked. "Well, Shantay told me about what happened at the quote-unquote Bible study."

I confirmed, "I didn't want to say nothin' to you about it 'cause I spoke my peace before they left."

"Good," she said. "When you think Rev. Martin be ready to listen to us?"

I thought about Henrietta and a few others who might actually side with Rev. Dukes. "I reckon we ought to pray about it first, Ophelia. I don't want to do nothin' to split the church."

She sighed. "Yeah, you right about that. Pastor Phillips just got Geneva back to town, and she in hospice over at Highland Crossings. Last thing he need is to be worryin' about the church. He ain't no spring chicken, either. Got to watch out for his own stress, too."

This was the first I had heard about Geneva being back. "When you headin' to see her?"

"Plan to go in the morning. So many folks from the church done been by there already, you know."

I asked, "What you gon' take over?"

"Spaghetti and garlic bread. Enough for a few days. Eunice Henderson said they got a sitting area with couches, a refrigerator and microwave and all for the visitors. Can you take some chicken Wednesday?"

"Surely. Good night, Ophelia."

"Good night."

Before I went to bed, me and Jesus had a long talk over a nice, tall glass of lemonade and the book of James. I ate the word like it was my dinner because, that night, it was.

After Libby and I finished our mid-week walk, she come back to my house and we made enough chicken, corn, and green beans to feed Pastor and Geneva for a few days. Packed some extra in plastic containers so he could freeze some for later. Then we hopped into my car and drove straight to Highland Crossings. Before we could even get down the hallway, I saw Eunice and Rev. Martin standing by Geneva's door.

"How y'all doing?" I asked them both.

"Fine," Eunice replied, looking at Libby like she out of place.

"Y'all remember Libby. First lady of First Baptist."

"Oh, yes." Eunice's face relaxed.

Libby asked, "Is it okay to go in?"

"Yes, go ahead," Rev. Martin said, holding the door open for me and Libby.

We made our way to the inner room. Now, I done seen plenty folk on their deathbeds, holdin' on for reasons only them and God know. I took a look at Geneva, her eyes all sunk in, her skin thin as onion paper, and nearly as white. Unless the Lord intervened, it wouldn't be too long. I don't know what they done to her at that cancer center, but it sure hadn't helped. Pastor did the right thing by bringing her back.

He was sitting right next to her bed, holding onto her hand like if he let go, she might fly away. Wasn't too long before, Pastor lost his mother. She was in her nineties, but it really don't matter how long somebody gets to live—still hurts when they die. Especially your momma.

"Hi Pastor," I whispered so as not to scare him.

"Mama B. Should have known you'd be here so quickly." He struggled to get to his feet. Pastor looked weak, too. I wondered if he even ate the food Ophelia brought him earlier up in the week.

"Yes, Lord. So good to see you, Pastor." He and I hugged, then I stepped aside so Libby could hug him, too.

Pastor started to thank her again for letting us use their sanctuary, but Libby waved him off. "Don't even think twice about it. I had my children share things all the time. I reckon God's no different."

Pastor offered his chair, but neither of us would take it. I don't know about Libby, but I was afraid he would keel over if he stood too long.

Geneva made a moaning sound, and all three of us rushed to her bedside. Her eyes rolled open for just a second. Then she said real soft like a song, "Mama B. Libby."

"Geneva, you decided to come back to Texas, I see," Libby joked.

"Somebody gotta. Take care Ed."

We all laughed a bit, glad to see her sense of humor still in place. Just like her to try and keep everybody else going. She was a first lady through and through.

"How's the church?" Geneva wanted to know.

Lord, I didn't want to say anything off-color. "We doin' fine, Geneva. Just fine."

Easy enough.

But Pastor Phillips pushed, "I've been asking Rev. Martin to give me tapes of the sermon, but he said the system at First Baptist wasn't set up to record sermons."

Libby squinted her eyes. "Oh, yes we are. I thought for sure Peter told Rev. Martin how to do it. I'll double-check."

Right there was my first inclination that maybe Rev. Martin didn't want Pastor Phillips hearin' Rev. Dukes messages because I know Peter told Rev. Martin how to tape the messages. I was sitting right there, heard it with my very own ears.

Somebody rapped on the door. "Knock knock."

"Come on in, Dr. Wilson," Pastor told him.

In walked the doctor. Tall, gray hair around the edges, and black as midnight. I thought maybe he was African until he said, "Hello, everyone," with no accent.

We all said hello back, including Geneva.

"May I have a moment with Miss Geneva? I need to take a good look at her."

"Yes, sir," Pastor answered, leading me and Libby out to the hallway.

"What the doctors been sayin'?" Eunice wanted to know.

Pastor frowned up. "They don't know. One minute they say all they can do is make her comfortable. Next minute, they want to try some experimental procedures. Insurance won't pay for it, no guarantee it'll work anyway. I don't want 'em using her for a guinea pig, but I want to give her every chance."

I patted his arm. "Doctors don't know everything, Pastor. That's why they in *practice*."

"Ain't that the truth," he agreed.

"Let's just pray right now," Libby said. She grabbed both our hands and we made a circle outside Geneva's room and called on Jesus. Thanked Him for His healing power, put our faith in His blood and His finished work on the cross. Asked the Lord to give the doctors wisdom, and give Pastor strength to continue aiding Geneva in Jesus's name.

We said, "Amen," and that's when I heard Dr. Wilson say it, too. Guess he joined in the prayer somewhere along the way.

"No change in her condition, but she is resting fairly well. You can go back in now."

"Thank you," Pastor said and he rushed back into the room.

Libby barely caught the door handle behind him.

That's when Dr. Wilson stopped in his tracks, turned back around and said to me, "Excuse me. I don't believe I caught your name."

"Beatrice."

"It's nice to meet you, Beatrice." Got a big, wide smile on his face. I, for one, didn't see much to be all chippy about. And for two, I know those teeth of his wasn't real.

"Thank you. Same here, Dr. Wilson. You take good care of my friend."

"Certainly. And I hope to see you again." He folded up his laptop and went on down the hallway.

We went back into the room, stood over Geneva with Pastor and sent up another prayer, then Libby pulled one of the plastic containers out of her purse and left it with Pastor. "We got plenty more where that came from. Just let B know when you and Geneva get home. We got 'em already frozen for you."

"Sure appreciate you and Libby," he said.

"Mmm hmm," Geneva moaned again.

Libby and I decided to make a little stop at the whole food store on the way back. Plenty fresh strawberries, blueberries, and green beans to choose from. I picked up a few squash. Cameron didn't know it yet, but he was about to float into squash heaven by the time I finished cooking it.

We got in line, waited our turn to check out. Libby come teasin' me, "Well, B, if I'm not mistaken, I do believe Dr. Wilson was a little sweet on you."

"Sweet on me?"

"Yes! He asked you for your name directly."

I smacked my lips. "Libby, that man wasn't studyin' me."

"Yes he most certainly was!"

"Well, if he was, I wouldn't know." I turned my nose up.

"Oh, B, why wouldn't he? Look at you." She held her arm out, swung her hand up and down like she showing off a washing machine on *The Price is Right*.

I looked past her. "Move ahead, Libby. You holdin' up the line."

Chapter 15

Cameron finished all his books before the due date, and Nikki said she would take him back to get more. "While I'm there, I can follow up on a job I applied for online last week. I can't believe you don't have an Internet connection in this house, Mama B."

"Hey, I got an iPhone with my email, and I can look stuff up on my phone. That's all I need," I said to her while cutting cantaloupe. That Cameron was a fruit fanatic, eat it all day if you don't watch him.

Nikki kissed me on the cheek. "It's alright. I need ta get that book *No Ways Tired* and read it before Saturday's book club meeting."

I smiled at her. "Nikki-Nik, you readin' books now?"

"Yes, if it's something I'm interested in." She slung her purse over her shoulder.

"Here. Taste this." I held out a piece of the fruit on a fork.

She winced. "No. I don't like cantaloupe."

"Try it and see." I pushed it closer to her mouth.

She closed her eyes, all dramatic, and bit into the sample. Her eyes opened, face brightened. "Wow, that was good!"

I winked at her. "You got to get it fresh from the farmer's market, not the big grocery store."

She rinsed her hands, grabbed a paper towel and stole a few more cubes from the bowl. "I'll see you later."

"Alright. I'm looking forward to this book you're bringing home. Maybe if you finish reading it early enough, I might get a few pages in before y'all meet so I can talk, too. That title is one of my favorite songs."

Rev. Martin didn't return none of my text messages or emails that week. Well, let me take that back. He didn't return 'em at a *decent hour*. Look like he waited 'til he knew good and well I was in bed with my phone turned off before he replied. Even then, he didn't answer my question. I wanted to know if me, him, a few of the deacons, and Ophelia could sit down that week. Discuss our concerns.

All he kept writing was he had to get in touch with so-and-so, and this one here on vacation, got to wait a little longer. Just stalling while the church go untended. Couldn't blame him all that much. Since the church air conditioner was still out, not like there was much meeting going on anyway. Ha! Seem like everybody took a break from meeting except all the folks who needed to meet at my house.

Well, we couldn't get the deacons together, but the Mother's Board come over early Friday afternoon. Me, Ophelia, Henrietta, and the oldest mother, Ruby Simon. Mother Simon really not always in her right mind since she had the stroke back in '09, but me and Ophelia make it our business to make sure Mother Ruby always at the meetings 'cause...well, mostly 'cause we hope people don't throw us away when we get old. You reap what you sow.

I don't know what on earth possessed Henrietta to invite one of the women from the Dukes' bunch to our Mt. Zion meeting, but here come some woman in a bright yellow muumuu and some 1980's jellies walkin' up my porch steps with Henrietta. Not the kind of jellies that's done came back in style. I mean, she had been havin' them actual shoes for over thirty years.

Lord, forgive me for judgin'. This ain't the Christ in me. I wasn't so much upset about the shoes as I was her being there. But that wasn't her fault, either. That was Henrietta's doing. I'm sure she put two and two together and figured out why I left church Sunday. She must have known this Mother's Board meeting wasn't gonna be in Pastor Dukes' favor, so she brought somebody along to be in her corner.

"B, This here is Mother Dorcas Powell. She want to join our Mother's Board."

She got to join our church, first. "Morning, Mother Powell. You welcome to sit in."

"Thank you, B. You have a lovely home." She looked me up and down first, then checked out my drapes, even craned her neck to get a look down a hallway we was not going to visit.

"Bless God," was all I could say.

Mother Powell hobbled on past me, but I caught Henrietta's arm and whispered to her, "She's not a member of Mt. Zion."

Henrietta snatched her arm away. "So long as Pastor Phillips is out, we got to make it our business to be hospitious to Pastor Dukes's church members."

I clenched my teeth. "He ain't got no church."

"Far as I'm concerned, he ought to have a church, or stay and help Pastor Phillips. Since he been preachin', I done won on almost every lotto ticket—at least a dollar every time. Last week, twenty-five! You can't tell me God haven't changed my luck on account of Rev. Dukes."

My Momma used to tell me all the time, "Book of Proverbs say you can't argue with foolishness." She was right, and I know the word is right, so I didn't say anything else to Henrietta on the matter. Just led her right on into the living room and served her fruit pizza right along with everybody else.

Ophelia had her yellow legal pad ready to take notes soon as she finished with the prayer. She and I had already discussed some things for the agenda, including prayer for Geneva and Pastor, so she started with those items. Then she got to what was chewin' on both our minds.

"Mothers, B and I wanted to lead a special prayer for our church body, and also discuss the direction the church is going since Pastor Phillips has been out on leave of absence," Ophelia said. She real good at saying stuff in a way where people won't get so mad— when she tryin' to be nice.

Henrietta sat up, squared her shoulders. "What direction you mean, Ophelia?"

"I mean in the direction of preaching the scriptures out of proper context or preaching with no scriptures at all," she explained real proper-like.

"I, for one, think Rev. Dukes is doing a great job. We got more new people visiting than we ever had," Henrietta said.

"But some of our *regular* members are skipping *out*," Ophelia opposed. "Including my own niece, Shantay, and her husband."

Henrietta mumbled, "One monkey don't stop the show."

"What you say?" Ophelia asked, turning her head to the side.

I jumped in, "Well, the purpose of our gathering is to pray and to figure out how to speak our peace with the deacon's board."

"I got nothing to say to them," again from Henrietta. "Rev. Dukes word workin' for me."

"Always work for me, too," Mother Powell added.

I decided to ask our visitor, "Mother Powell, you more familiar with Rev. Dukes than the rest of us. How long you been under his teaching?"

"'Bout two years, since the Lord brought me back in. I spent most of my life doing my own thing—in the clubs, drinking, and smoking. But my daughter started going to church, and she brought me. I heard Pastor Dukes preaching and teaching on the abundant life. Now I go to her church every time I see Pastor Dukes is preaching on the calendar."

"Your life is certainly a wonderful testimony," I had to admit. It's always better to be in the church than in the club.

Henrietta nodded.

I worked up to my real question. "So maybe you can answer this for me. Do he always preach about money and how to get what you want from the Lord? Do he have other things he preach on like, for instance, the fruit of the Spirit?"

"Naw. He don't talk about food too much."

Mother Simon sniggered. First peep we heard out of her all day.

"How about holiness? Serving the Lord with your life?"

She shook her head 'no.' "He don't preach on stuff like that, and I'm glad 'cause I would probably be nodding off in church!" She laughed so big her cheekbones nearly made her eyes shut closed.

Nobody but her and Henrietta thought that was funny. I was beginning to wonder if Mother Powell was a church mother or if maybe she was just *Rev. Dukes'* mother.

When she finally realized the rest of us didn't find respond to her joke, she straightened up her face. "Listen, I know what you're trying to say. You all don't like Rev. Dukes. Y'all think he ain't good enough for your church."

"Nobody's saying we don't like Rev. Dukes," Ophelia corrected her.

"No, hear me out." Mother Powell put up her hand like a stop-sign in Ophelia's direction.

All I could do was pray to the Lord for a split-second 'cause one thing I know about Ophelia: she slow to get angry, but once she get there, she definitely there.

"All he doing is trying to get us all to a point where we not struggling anymore. Robbing Peter to pay Paul, choosing between paying for medications or the water bill every month. But by the looks of your house and your high-dollar clothes, and all your kids' certificates and degrees and so on, I see you can't understand where the rest of us coming from."

Once again, Henrietta hissed under her breath, "You sure right about that."

I realized I didn't have to answer to either one of them, but, you know, once somebody drag your kids into the situation, now we got a *real* problem on our hands. "Mother Powell, I'll have you to know my husband and I didn't have the best education or the best background, but we put God first in everything, and He honored His word. All this you see and all the blessings you *don't* see, we got by His grace. *That's* how real prosperity works."

Mother Powell shook her head and declared, "Not in my book."

"What book *you* readin'?" I asked. Soon as the question left my lips, the Holy Spirit whispered inside me, *that's enough.*

He must have said the same thing to Ophelia. She stood up and held out both arms. "Ladies, let's close in prayer."

I grabbed Ophelia's hand on the right. Didn't have no choice but to grab Henrietta's on the left.

Ophelia prayed. "Father, You are perfect in all Your ways. Show us Your ways and let us line up with them. And now as we depart, we thank You in advance for Your protection, which You promised in Your word to all who would abide under Your mighty shadow. Help us to abide there. It's in Your precious Son Jesus' name we pray, amen."

"Amen."

Shame how fast everybody cleared out. Usually, we all sit around talking and laughing. Not this time, though. Henrietta and Mother Powell left while Ophelia was still getting Mother Simon situated in the car.

Once Mother Simon's seatbelt was buckled, Ophelia closed the car door and said to me, "Well, the Mother's Board can't go to the deacon's board divided."

"Sure can't. May be just me and you on behalf of all the folk that's done already stopped coming to church, and some of the other ones that's just waitin' it out."

"Or maybe we should just wait Rev. Dukes out," she suggested. "May not be too long before God move one way or another for Geneva."

I took a deep breath. "I hear you, sister, I hear you. May be the best thing, God willing, for us to wait and see."

Chapter 16

After all that nonsense with Henrietta and Mother Powell, I really didn't feel like having the book club meeting at my house. The church "theft investigation" was complete, according to Dustin. We were innocent, of course. Now, it was just a matter of the usual estimating and processing and whatnot before they cut the check. Might take the bank a day or two to release the funds.

My thinking was to postpone the book club meeting until they could take it back to Dukes territory. But when I told Libby a little about my feelings, she recommended I didn't change things. "Now, B, remember you don't want to be the cause of strife and revenge. God ain't in that."

I followed her advice and kept my word about hosting.

Nikki could hardly wait to start the meeting. Much as her nose had been buried between the pages of *No Ways Tired*, I knew she would have a lot to say. She had her library copy sitting front and center on the coffee table like a centerpiece when the ladies arrived.

Seem like Cynthia had calmed down. She hugged me and kissed me when she walked in, thanked me again for allowing them to meet. I was glad, too. Last thing I wanted was another hostile situation in my home.

Not as many people came to the book club meeting as the "Bible study." Too bad, though, 'cause I sure put my foot in that potato salad.

"Mama B, I have not had potato salad this good since my family reunion two years ago," one of the girls from the other congregation praised. "You must give me the recipe."

"Honey, I don't have no recipe. You'll have to come watch me make it one of these days."

Karen hummed, "Mmmm mmm. That's the best kind of cooking."

This time, Karen opened up the group with the prayer. Then she shuffled through her giant purse for a second, finally putting her hand on her book. "Okay. Y'all, this book was soooo good. I could not stop reading it!"

"Me, either," Nikki cooed. "I have never read anything so real. I mean, this is how black people act, for real!"

I sat back in the love seat, pleased to hear my granddaughter gushin' over a book. I knew the more she read, the more Cameron would read. Kids don't do what you say, they do what you *do*.

Since I hadn't been able to pry the book out of Nikki's hands, I planned to listen to the conversation and decide if I wanted to read it for myself later on.

"I was caught up in the first chapter." Karen smiled and flipped a few pages while everyone else followed suit. She ran her finger along the side of a page and started readin' out loud. "If my husband knew what I knew, he wouldn't spend so many hours at the gym trying to get buff. He wouldn't spend so much time at the office trying to get rich. In fact, if he had a clue about what I do while he's trying to keep up with the Jones's, he'd bring his behind home. But I wouldn't want him home because then he'd keep me from Pastor

Flexner. I got to have me some Pastor Flexner at least three times a week."

"Oooh wee!" Jada Sutton nearly screamed. "When I read that part, I was like—man! She's sleeping with the pastor?"

The air left my chest. "Lord, have mercy."

All of 'em laughed at me like my reaction was just so funny.

"Well, it does happen," Karen said, dipping her chin in Jada's direction. "Pastors *do* cheat on their wives."

"My cousin is a pastor," Cynthia added, "and he had two or three children by other women."

"Did his wife ever leave him?" one of the ladies wanted to know.

"Never. He made too much money."

Nikki fanned through her copy. "I think that's why Maxine stayed. She must have known Pastor Flexner was cheating, but she didn't want to give up her lifestyle. Right here, on page two-hundred and thirteen, she says, all men cheat. So you might as well pick one with some money because no matter what, you're going to get played."

I tell you, my head was going side to side like I'm watching a tennis match. They talked about one crazy scene after another. And the more they talked, the more I wondered about this here book. I had to ask, "Well, did the pastor ever repent?"

"No!" They all said in unison.

Karen explained, "By the end of the book, his wife left him, but he's still preaching and looking for a new wife. He has not learned his lesson yet. That's why we have to read the next one."

Another young lady smiled. "I can hardly wait until part three comes out."

They got to talking about some of the other stuff going on in the book—all the folks the pastor was sleeping with, how he paid off the elders of the church to stay quiet, how one of the teens in the church was pregnant by the pastor but his wife paid for the girl to have an abortion, but the girl kept the money and she still pregnant. All that, I supposed, would get discussed in book three.

"But this was my favorite part," Jada spoke again. "When Maxine finally walked in on Pastor Flexner and her hairdresser." She found a spot in the book and read off a tell-everything love-making scene followed by a whole bunch of choice words I can't even repeat.

Look like they done made up some new cussword-matches, 'cause some of them combinations I hadn't never heard before that night.

Guess I got the church book club to thank for adding those to my vocabulary.

Chapter 17

Just like the last time, all I could do was steal away from the meeting and make myself busy with something else in the kitchen. Nobody really invited me to the club anyway, no rule saying I had to stay and sit up and listen to them talk about a man of God—even if he wasn't real. Dangerous territory, if you ask me. God don't like folks makin' a joke about His kids any more than you want folks to paint a likeness of your kids and start talkin' bad about 'em. Even if they is wrong.

I know it was just a make-believe book. But still. Kind of like I thought the Bible study was supposed to be upliftin' and pointing toward godly things, looked like the same thing was goin' on with the "church" book club.

After I nit-picked all the little cleaning jobs in my kitchen and dusted from my room to the front parlor, the meeting was over. Apparently, the women liked that book so much, they decided to read six more books from that same author. Said they was gonna focus on her the rest of the year.

Karen closed the gathering in prayer, and most of them left in one big swoop. Only Karen, Cynthia, Nikki, and I were left.

"Mama B, you can read my copy now," Nikki said as she put the last of my magazines back in place.

"That's alright, Nikki-Nik. You can take it back to the library tomorrow." God is my witness, that's all I said. This is a free country. Folks free to read whatever they want.

Promise to God, I was planning on keeping my mouth shut and ridin' it out 'til Pastor Phillips came back. That's what me and Ophelia agreed to. Plus, since God hadn't said too much to me about this whole church situation in a while, I figured all this with Rev. Dukes and book clubs was just meant to show that the Mothers and I needed to spend more time with the younger women in the church.

Then Cynthia—almost out the door, had her foot on the silver part between my wood and the porch—stopped and asked me, "You didn't like the book?"

I shrugged my shoulders real quick and sort. "Don't sound like something I would be interested in."

She drug her foot back inside and let the screen door close. "Mama B, forgive me, but I really thought this book club would be an opportunity to make up for our misunderstanding last time."

I'm not the one with the misunderstanding. Before I said another word, I had to think: *am I mad?* A little. Sad probably a better word, though. Took my mind a second to push aside the mad thoughts and decide on words to bring us toward a solution.

I walked over toward the doorway, Nikki and Karen behind me at that point. "Cynthia, I know you're trying to reach the church women, trying to encourage them to do more with their lives, to read—"

"You're exactly right. So why did you walk out of the room with a frown on your face during the book discussion? If I didn't know any better, I'd think you're trying to undermine everything I do. Are you jealous? Upset because I can get the women do get together but you can't?"

Karen's hand come into my side-vision. She touched Cynthia's arm. "Sister, don't."

Cynthia pulled away. "No, I'm tired of this. What is the problem, Mama B?"

"Well, right now, my problem is you disrespecting me in my own house." I warned her with my eyes she that better watch her mouth.

She clicked her cheek. "I'm sorry."

I could see a little pool forming in her eyes. "Apology accepted."

She blinked a few times. "What's wrong with church women meeting up, spending social time together? If the world can do it, so can we."

"I got no problem with church women meeting up. God *started* the idea of fellowship when he created Adam, so the world is copyin' *us*. And I'm sure God don't mind seein' his daughters get together."

In a tiny voice, Karen asked, "So what's the issue? We want to know what you think we're doing wrong. I mean, it *is* a Christian book." She stood next to Cynthia.

Nikki must have stayed in her place because I didn't hear her feet move.

Even though Cynthia didn't seem like she wanted an explanation, Karen did. So, for her sake, I continued, "You think maybe y'all could have picked a book with a little less cussin' or maybe with some kind of hope and encouragement for the people of God? This book sound like it come straight from the world. Just 'cause they slapped a gospel song title and a preacher on the cover don't make it *Christian*."

Cynthia pushed her bangs off her eyebrow. "We read books that keep it *real*, not fairytales. And besides, we try to support black authors."

"Cynthia, I got one question for you. In all this business-meetin' you doin' with church folk, and all this book-readin' you got going on with the church ladies, where is Jesus?"

She looked at me like I had a tree growing out of my head. "He's here, with *us*, when we meet. The Bible says where two or three are gathered, He's in the midst."

I shook my head. "Bible says where two or three are gathered together *in My name*. Big difference between gathering for His glory and gathering together for something else. You think Jesus would have enjoyed being in the midst tonight, listening to all that bad language y'all was readin'? All those strong love-making scenes the single girls got to try to forget about the next time they out on a date? You think Jesus would have enjoyed listening to y'all laugh about how bad pastors can be? Wonder if He thinks it's funny for His body to be in such bad shape?"

Karen's jaw dropped open. Light bulb must have went off in her head.

Nikki piped up, "Mama B, I mean, seriously, it's a *novel*." She walked over and stood on the other side of Cynthia, facing me now. "It's only *entertainment*. They're just words on a page. Just words."

"That's precisely what the enemy *wants* you to think."

Karen said, almost in a whisper, "Thank you for bringing this to mind. And thanks, again, for letting us meet here." She tapped Cynthia's shoulder.

Cynthia unfroze and they both walked out.

Nikki shut the door behind them and stomped off to her temporary bedroom.

Chapter 18

Thank God, the church air finally got fixed. I know everybody was happy, but I was double-happy 'cause all them women's meetings was 'bout to wear me out. Not just Cynthia's, either. The usher board, the nurses. Cooking class came back again. Goin' by the calendar, it had only been a matter of weeks. Goin' by my nerves, months had went by.

Maybe because Nikki and Cameron were there, too. Nikki had done went on three interviews in a row one day, and she felt pretty good about every last one. "Cameron and I will be out of your hair pretty soon."

They weren't any trouble, really. Only time I had to get onto Cameron was when he left his shoes here and there. At first, we had a little problem with him wetting the bed. Nikki fussed at him, but I told her that's how little boys—and some big boys—do. They bladders sometimes slow to catch up with they bodies. Got to stop their liquids early in the evening if you don't want no accidents.

Rosetta Eaglefoot, down the street, had two grandsons around Cameron's age came over to spend some time with her for the summer. Once Cameron found out about them, we didn't hardly see him none through the day. The boys played indoor games and whatnot at Rosetta's house. Then, 'round six or so, the three of 'em, plus some more kids must be visiting, come racing up and down the street on bicycles and playing baseball. Cameron came home every night stinking like a hog, hungry as a cow. He ate, took his bath, and fell off to sleep like he been working on the railroad all day.

For the most part, Nikki wasn't no problem, either, except Libby and I come home from helping at the food pantry one day and heard Nikki on my house phone cussin' up a storm like *she* wrote the book they was reading at that wild book club meeting two weeks prior.

Oh, I mean, she was going at it. Didn't know we had stepped in the front door, evidently. Tell you, she was callin' somebody everything but a child of God.

"Nikki! Watch your mouth!" I fussed, clapping my hands with every word.

Shock all on her face. She slammed the phone down. "Oh, Mama B and Miss Libby, I am so sorry. I am sooo sorry."

Libby made light of it. "I ain't heard cussin' like that since Peter was in the navy."

"Please forgive me, Miss Libby."

"What you cussin' like that for, anyway?" I asked her.

"It's J.T. Ooh! I can't stand him! He had my phone turned off."

I asked, "Was he payin' the bill?"

"No. Actually, I was paying *both* our cell phone bills."

"Now, I know you got more sense than that," I snapped.

"We were both on the same plan, *my* plan, but he used to pay it when we were together. When we broke up, I only had two more months left before I could drop him without an early termination fee, so I decided to go ahead and keep him on until August. I don't know what

J.T. did, but somehow he turned off both our phones, plus I have a five hundred dollar disconnection penalty!"

Libby gave Nikki a slight smile. "Well, at least you got a reason for being mad as a hornet."

Nikki took a deep breath and sank down to the couch, covering her hands with her face.

I asked, "What phone company was you with?"

"P-R Wireless."

"Hmph. Well, your Aunt Debra Kay works for Junction Connections. Maybe if you give her a call right quick, she can get you another phone and another line."

Nikki didn't look up. "But all the places I put in applications with have *this* cell phone number and the email address tied to *this* account." She pointed to the worthless plastic and glass on the table. "If somebody was trying to call me today and give me an offer, I wouldn't even know."

Libby pressed, "Hon, you think if you called him back, you two could talk it out?"

Nikki shook her head. "He's unreasonable. He says the only way he'll turn it back on is if I come back to him."

"Don't sound like a good option to me," I advised her. "Anybody that spiteful got a serious problem."

She hopped up from the couch and grabbed her purse. "I'm going to the library to create a new email account and send it to the places I know have an interest in me."

Libby and I watched Nikki walk out the door, then looked at each other.

"She sure is a go-getter," Libby gave a compliment. "Just like her grandmother."

That same day, me and Libby went to visit Geneva again. We had packed plenty food for Pastor, but we just missed him. Instead, Deacon Bledsoe, LaTonya, and one of Geneva's nieces were sitting up with her. They said Pastor had gone back to the house to get a change of clothes.

By this time, they had done moved Geneva to another wing of the building. Real quiet in that hallway. Time was winding down fast for Geneva, Pastor had told us the week before. Said she wasn't really eating much. Had a hard time swallowing. And she was going in and out of consciousness.

Just so happen, she was woke when me and Libby come to either side of her bed that day. "Geneva?"

She barely opened her eyes. "B." Her voice was scratchy, scarcely there.

"Yes, it's me. And Libby Maxwell." Me and Libby leaned in real close. "We came by to see you and give Pastor some food."

"Mmmm. Thank."

"Don't try to talk, hon," Libby said. "Keep your energy."

"Won't need it."

I checked her arms to see if the medicine might be talking for her, but she didn't have no tubes. "Geneva, don't talk like that. You got a lot more left to do. You ain't but sixty-three years old."

"Jeez wuh thirty-three."

Libby giggled. "You sure right, hon, and He saved the whole world in His lifetime."

Geneva raised her arm slightly. "Mmm hmmm. Saw him."

"Saw who?"

"Him." She swallowed. "High. Liff-ed up." A peaceful grin come cross her face for a second. "I'm ready."

A tear escaped from my eye and landed on her arm. I hoped she didn't feel it.

"No worryin'. Won't be long. Time diff'rent there," her voice creaked to a stop.

Libby kissed Geneva on the forehead. "B, I'll meet you outside. Good-bye, Geneva."

"Mmmm hmmm."

Libby left the room before her own tears showed. She wasn't too good with death right then seeing as her own Momma just passed away the year previous.

I know that feelin' too.

I hurt for Pastor, for us all. Live long enough, and you'll be at somebody's bedside near the end, right before the heart rest or the family decide to turn off the machines. Everything get real clear then.

I had been beside more than one person say they done had a taste of the other side. None of 'em want to come back, and by what I done read in the Bible, I can't rightly blame 'em.

So I got real close again. "Hold on, Geneva. Long as you can. God is a healer. But if you want to go, we'll understand."

Her lips trembled. "Ed."

"Like you said, he'll be there before you know it. All of us will."

She tapped at my finger with the little power she had left.

Now, I ain't no superstitious woman and I don't believe in ghosts and all that stuff. But I done read in the Bible where the rich man saw Lazarus, so it sound to me like dead peoples can recognize each other. If Geneva was on her way to heaven...I know it's selfish...but I had to ask her a favor. "Geneva. If you see my Albert...tell him I said hello."

She gave me her last grin. "Affa Jeez."

I couldn't help but laugh. "Yes, *after* you talk to Jesus."

Chapter 19

My hair appointment ran long, but Libby said she'd wait for me at the midtown café. Good thing, too, 'cause I sure needed to pray with her. Those women at the beauty shop gave me an earful about my own church!

"The Pastor's wife is on her last leg, and the new pastor is going to take over soon. Some people don't like the new pastor, but they mostly old biddies. Just want to keep the church from moving on." Naomi Jester—a woman who went to high school with my late husband, which made her way too old to be gossiping like that—told everybody.

Well, wasn't but three beauty operators and me and Naomi in the salon. Come to a total of five people, but Naomi toutin' this story like she done practiced it a few times.

"At Mt. Zion?" my hairdresser, Kendra echoed.

Naomi confirmed, "Yes, at *Mt. Zion!*"

Kendra finished rolling a section of my hair. "Isn't that your church, Mama B?"

"Sure is." I said it loud enough for Naomi to hear. She knew that. *Had* to know. She was must have been hoping I would give her some more information to add to the story.

"Whose side you on, B?" Naomi asked, leaning toward me, just waiting for me to drop a morsel of sin.

"Ain't no *sides.*"

"Ouch!" Naomi squealed.

"Miss Naomi, you have to sit still while I'm pressing your hair."

Served her right.

Nobody but Libby I would go to about something like this. Ophelia was good aboutkeepin' her cool and keepin' down confusion in a meeting. But if and when she get to talkin' on the phone a lot, sometimes things slipped out. Not saying anything bad about her. That's just the way it is. The more you talk, bigger chance something get said that don't need to be said.

Anyhow, Libby the kind of friend who know how to shut her mouth even if mine happen to keep runnin'. And I do the same to her when I have to 'cause ain't neither one of us perfect.

I tell you what, though, I didn't hardly make it into the café good when I seen who sittin' at the table with her. None other than Dr. Wilson! He had on a white, starched button-down shirt and blue jeans with some big cowboy boots.

Libby smilin' from ear to ear in her pink sundress. They talkin', laughin' when I walked up to the table.

"Hey, B! Look who I found," Libby very nearly sang to me. She motioned toward him with her hand like she one of them models showin' off a prize on The Price is Right. "You remember Dr. Wilson?"

"Yes, I do. How are you, Dr. Wilson?"

"Fine," he said. He stood up to shake my hand. I noticed his eyes were a lighter shade of brown than I remembered. And then I wondered why I would remember something so silly anyway.

"I was just keeping Libby company until you got here."

"Oh, there's no need to rush," from Libby. Her silvery-blonde hair bounced at the curled-up ends while she nodded for me to agree.

I didn't.

Now, I know Peasner a small, friendly town and all, but Libby had done took it too far, in my opinion. I drawed up my eyes and looked at her real quick. She shrugged her shoulders like she Miss Innocent.

Dr. Wilson showed all thirty-two of his teeth and peered all in my face. "B, Libby was telling me that you—"

"It's Beatrice." *He don't know me like that.* I took my seat.

"I apologize. *Beatrice*, Libby was telling me that the two of you volunteer at the food pantry. You must know my daughter, Eva. She volunteers there, too, some weekends."

I tipped my head. "Yes, I do know her. Lovely young lady. You must be proud of her."

"Very. She's finishing up her master's degree in education."

"Wonderful. Well, it was nice seeing you again."

Libby kicked my foot under the table. I glanced up at her and she—what Cameron call it?—*mean-mugging* me. I did it back to her while Dr. Wilson was busy looking down at his cell phone.

"Forgive me, ladies. I have to take this call." He held the phone to his ear, got up, and walked outside. Probably the only place to get good reception.

"B, what in the world is wrong with you?"

I fussed, "Why you got this man sittin' here at our table?"

Waitress come over and took our order in the middle of the debate. We picked up right where we left off.

"Ain't no harm in having somebody else join us for lunch, is it?" she asked like she had no idea.

"Dr. Wilson ain't just *somebody*. You said he was sweet on me, and the way he starin' all in my eyeballs when he talk. I don't like it. I think he flirtin' with me."

"He *is* flirtin' with you, B. Still don't see the problem."

I took a sip of ice water. "I ain't on the market."

"You single, ain'tcha?"

"I'm *widowed*. Besides, he way too young for me."

"Oh, B, Dr. Wilson got to be at least sixty-five."

"And I'm seventy-two. Seven years gap between us."

"At our age, I don't think seven years gon' make you a tiger, B."

Couldn't help but laugh. "I think they call it a cougar."

Libby shook her head and squeezed a lemon into her glass. "Tiger, cougar, leopard, whatever. You ain't it. Besides, I think he's rather tall, dark and handsome."

"Libby, you ain't no good judge of black men. Dr. Wilson ain't near handsome as Albert was."

She dipped her chin almost to her neckline. "Honey, nobody gon' be able to compare with Albert. You fell in love with him before he lost all his hair and got wrinkles. But I think you ought to at least open your mind up enough to make new friends, be it Dr. Wilson, or whoever."

I tilted my head to the side and gave way to the rumble of laughter in my belly. "Libby, what I look like makin' friends with a man at this point in my life?"

"B, it's not—"

"No, listen. Let's say I start courtin' a man. How long you think we got to get to know each other and get a relationship goin'?"

She looked me square in the face. "No two people know how long they gon' have together, no matter what age they are. Like Geneva said, won't be long before we all on the other side. Just got to be thankful for every day."

Sometimes, people say stuff that just sink right inside your heart. I swallowed real hard 'cause I know Libby know what she talkin' about. Her first husband died in a work accident two weeks after they got married. They was both only nineteen years old at the time. She hadn't even had time for a groove to set in on her ring finger before he was gone. "I hear you, Libby."

Dr. Wilson come back at the same time the waitress brought our food. "I apologize again, Libby and Beatrice, but I have to head to the hospital."

The waitress, a young lady with a long, brunette ponytail that almost hit her behind, asked him, "Did you want to order something to go?" That girl wanted her tip, I see.

"No, thank you. But I'll take their check." Dr. Wilson motioned toward me and Libby.

Me and Libby both pushed our backs against our chairs, turned toward each other real slow. Probably looked like we had done rehearsed it.

"Why, thank you, Dr. Wilson," Libby said first.

I added, "We certainly do appreciate it."

"My pleasure." He bowed a little at the waist. "Beatrice, I'd love to treat you to lunch again. Well," he stumbled, "both of you, if—"

"No need in me tagging along," Libby rescued him.

I do declare, beads of sweat popped out on Dr. Wilson's forehead while he waited for my answer. *He actually nervous.* "Yes, Dr. Wilson. I'll agree to lunch."

"Wonderful," he said. "May I have your phone number?"

"Let me give you my email address," I offered instead. *Got no time to be sittin' on the phone talkin' to no man.* I wrote my information on a napkin and handed it to him.

"Have a great day, Dr. Wilson," I sent him away.

"Frank."

I supposed if I had a fit about what I wanted him to call me by, I should oblige him as well. "Okay. Have a great day, *Frank*."

Chapter 20

After my visit with Geneva earlier in the week, I had no problem overlooking Rev. Dukes's sermons. Life too short to spend it worrying about what I think other people doin' wrong. I got my own stuff to deal with. Plus, since I started praying about it, the Lord hadn't said nothing one way or another. Sometimes, you just got to sit and let stuff work out in the spirit world before you know what's the next natural step to take. God'll tell you when to move.

Sunday morning, I kept my Bible handy (just in case) while Rev. Dukes talked on the importance of separating yourself from so-called "haters" and other people who don't want to see you get rich. Folk was cheerin' him on and runnin' 'round the building in circles.

But back to the hatin' part—I sat there wondering who in they right mind sit up thinking 'bout all the people who hate them? You know somebody hate you, you pray for them, treat them nice and keep right on movin'. Can't nobody stop you from pleasing God but yourself. Plus, you live long enough, you figure out folks ain't studyin' you near much as you think they are.

Like I said, I wasn't gon' raise no stink about things, though. We were five weeks into this drought with Rev. Dukes. I figured we were closer to the end of him than the beginning.

At the end of the service, one of Rev. Dukes' folks, young man by the name of Brandon, got up and made mention of a back-to-school talent show for the kids.

Well, since Shantay, her husband, and the other family that mostly work with the youth had been skippin' out on church in Pastor's absence, I was glad somebody stepped in. So long as the kids just sang their songs and did their praise dances, should have been fine.

Cameron ran hisself straight to the front of the church soon as we dismissed. Him and about ten more kids gathered around Brandon to sign up for the talent show.

Since he didn't need no ride to church, Cameron was the first one there at practice Monday evening, too. He must have told Rosetta's grandsons about it 'cause they all come stompin' through the house after Brandon let them out of practice. I mean, they was goin' at it.

Reminded me of Otha back when Albert and me went to see him perform with his fraternity. Chile, they was steppin' and movin' like we back in Africa! Thought they was doin' something new, I guess.

Same thing with Cameron. "You want to see our routine?"

I sat down on the sofa. "Sure. Go right ahead."

Rosetta's oldest grandson said, "Well, there will be seven of us stepping Friday night. But we'll do what we can."

"I understand."

Cameron and the other two boys line up in front of the television set. They counted off, "One. Two. One, two, three, four."

They only got about eight counts into the dance when somebody messed up. Don't know which one it was, but they had to start over. Twice.

Finally, Cameron gave up. "Never mind, Mama B. We'll go outside and work on it some more."

Tickled me, but I didn't laugh none 'cause they was serious about this thing. "Good idea. Y'all go on outside, I'll make you some snacks for after you finish. I can hardly wait to see the performance Friday night."

They traipsed out there and practiced the moves. Rosetta's grandsons almost got into a fight, but Cameron intervened. Little peacemaker, that boy was. Make any father or grandfather proud.

I fished my cell phone from my purse and sent Son another text.

Your grandson performing at church Friday night.

Few minutes later, he returned.

Sorry. Can't make it. Plans already.

Plans, my foot. I could see I was going to have to practice the Rule of One on Son. Something I hadn't done with him since Nikki was born.

Me and Libby come up with the Rule of One. It's when you got grown kids and they don't want to listen to you and you already know a face-to-face meetin' won't really get you nowhere 'cause somebody always got to have the last word.

Instead of a conversation, write a letter and tell 'em one time and one time only about what's on your heart. Give them advice. In love. Let 'em know this the *only* time you gon' bring it up, 'less they want to talk about it (that's the "One" part).

When Jesus talked to folks, He didn't sit there arguing. He might say "Do you want to be healed?" or "I am the Son of God" and that was it. They either believed or they didn't. Ain't got time to sit up trying to talk people to death. Talk don't help some people.

Other thing about the rule is: you can't do it often. Some kids, never. Some kids two or three times in a lifetime. Only when you see they gettin' ready to do something you believe they gon' regret for a long, long time.

Last time I did the Rule of One with Son was when told me he was leavin' his family for Nikki's momma. Said he was bored with Wanda. Dianne made him feel "alive" again. Now, I couldn't figure out how he was feelin' dead already at the ripe old age of twenty-four. I *did* know what he *was* feelin', and *it* certainly wasn't dead.

Son got a good heart. Since him and Wanda got back together, he been doin' good with his family and his church. But, in the natural, he always been the kind who love to tell other people what they doin' wrong, yet don't like nobody to point out his faults. Can't stand to be wrong. We couldn't hardly play Monopoly with him 'cause he nearly fall out when he land on "Go to Jail!"

Anyhow, he still my son. I still had a right and a obligation to speak the truth into his life. Just had to figure out what words to say.

And I knew I wasn't the One with all the answers.

Chapter 21

I finished making the grilled sandwiches for Cameron and his summer buddies. Called them in to eat, then sent the other two home. I was planning on taking my shower first, but by the smell of him, I let him go ahead.

When Nikki come in, I called it a night. Left her to tend to her son while I tended to mine.

I met Jesus in the rocking chair. Pulled out my Bible and read first Corinthians chapter thirteen again. Reminded me of who I am in Christ before I wrote the Rule of One letter to Son. Not rude, not self-seeking, not proud, slow to anger.

Took me nearly an hour to write the letter. This was the one shot I had to let Son know exactly how I felt with no tit-for-tat. I wrote it on stationery Libby got me, with flowers and everything on it. Anything to help Son know how much I loved him, how much God loved him. Told him not to carry 'round the guilt of what happened between him and Nikki's momma. Nobody's perfect, but everybody been forgiven in Christ – past, present, and future. Time for him to move on, don't let the enemy steal the relationship with his grandson, especially. I expected Son would call me in a day or two, after he got the letter.

Now, I thought my last words would be to Jesus that night, but Nikki come knocking on the door.

"Mama B? You sleep?"

With the hallway light on, I could see her sliding her hands up and down the thigh part of her pants.

"What's the matter?" I switched on the night lamp.

She walked over and sat on the foot of my bed, shaking like a leaf. "I saw J.T.'s car."

"Where?"

"In my rearview mirror. He must have found your address by doing a reverse search on your landline after I called him."

Folks and all this technology. Stalkers ain't even got to work hard no more. "You want to call the police?"

"No. I've been through this with J.T. before. When he gets like this, he starts acting real crazy. I...I think maybe me and Cameron need to move back with him. I don't want to put you in any danger."

I sat up in my bed. "Nikki, is it something else you ain't told me?"

She dropped her head. My stomach dropped, too. All along, I knew there was something more to this story.

"J.T.'s cousin. The one I was working for?"

I nodded. "Yeah."

"Well. When I left. I took some things with me."

"Things like what?"

She blurted out, "Money."

One thing I know, people don't play about they money. One of Albert's best friends got shot over five dollars in a crap game.

"How *much* money?"

She squeaked, "Two thousand dollars."

My chest loosened a little. Guess I was thinking she'd say something higher. She should have been able to resolve this matter it soon as she got a job. "You need to pay it back."

"No, I don't."

I raised my brow at her.

She softened. "Well, not all of it. I know how J.T. and his cousin work. They were not about to give me my last two weeks' earnings. I'd have to get a lawyer, which would have cost me more than I'd earned. They always kept the last paycheck of everyone they fired. I wasn't going to let them get over on me like that, so I helped myself. Plus, now, J.T. owes me another five hundred dollars for the phone. I might owe them four hundred dollars, tops."

She had a point. "Maybe you should talk to J.T. See if y'all can't reason this out, like Libby said the other day. Sit down and put pencil to paper. Right is right. Figure out exactly what you *do* owe the business, and pay it back."

"J.T. is not a reasonable person. A reasonable person would have knocked on your door and asked to speak to me. We might have argued, I might have ended up calling the cops, but still, the whole thing would be reasonable. But J.T.'s the kind of person who would rather follow me and make me feel scared weeks and weeks before he actually does whatever it is he's going to do."

I had to ask. "Well, if he's so unreasonable, what were you doin' with him?"

She paused, like nobody ever asked her that before. "Good question."

"You got a good answer?"

She stopped again. "No ma'am."

Well, least she was honest. One thing I can say about my Nikki-Nik. She might do wrong, but she don't try to cover it up. When she called me and told me she was pregnant, she didn't make no excuses. So I knew she was telling the truth about the money. And about J.T.

Her foot started tapping against my floor. "What should I do, Mama B?"

"You remember that summer you came to stay with me and that girl stole your money from your backpack at the Y-M-C-A?"

"Yes, ma'am."

I pushed the covers off my chest. "We gon' do the same thing now we did then."

"Accept Christ again as my Ssavior?"

"No. You only need to do that once, so long as you believed. Right now, we gon' pray. Pray for J.T. Pray for you. Pray for the Lord to intervene."

She joined me on the side of the bed. We went before the Lord. Nikki asked Him to forgive her for taking the money. I asked the Lord to protect us all, and help her and J.T. come to an agreement.

When we got finished, she very nearly begged, "Can Cameron and I sleep in your room?"

Five minutes later, Cameron was nestled at the foot of my bed; Nikki leaned back in my rocking chair. They drifted off to sleep.

But the Holy Spirit wouldn't let me rest. He sent me through the house with my oil, anointing every doorknob, every window, speaking the word. "No weapon formed against us shall prosper."

Chapter 22

Most of the children spent Wednesday night in the fellowship hall while service went on in the sanctuary. They called theyself getting ready for their different acts for the talent show. Whole thing got throwed together real fast if you ask me, but didn't nobody ask me so I didn't say a word.

Me and Ophelia sat next to each other. Henrietta had done moved over to the other side with Mother Powell. They carried on as usual with Rev. Dukes doin' his thing, preaching on the topic of supporting black businesses. By this time, I say about half the women in the buildin' wearing that Body Enchantment. You can tell by the way they sittin' up straight, can't hardly breathe, with they bosom crawling up to they neck. Plus when they turn around, you see a big chunk of fat right under the armpit. Look to me like Body Enchantment don't do nothin' but push the fat around.

Again, I kept my mouth shut. Maybe I was one of the haters Rev. Dukes always preachin' about. Just seem like nothing but negativity come out of me lately when it come to the church. *I repent, Lord.*

Mother Powell must have been the only one without a Body Enchantment suit 'cause she got to shoutin' and—y'all ain't gone believe this—her stockings fell slamp to the ground! Most peoples was so busy carryin' on, they didn't see it, but I did.

She booked over and grabbed 'em real fast, tried to slide 'em up real quick. Lord, I like ta rolled of that pew laughing. *I repent again, Lord. Gimme some kind of compassion from somewhere.*

I knew then it was time for a fast. Cut back on feeding the flesh, give my spirit more to work with 'cause I couldn't keep going down this road with Mt. Zion. Even if Geneva let go soon, it would take Pastor a time to move on.

I got to do better. Can't be standing in the gap for my granddaughter while I got a big gap open in my own life.

While Nikki gabbed with Cynthia 'nem at the front of the church after the benediction, I made my way to the church kitchen to get Cameron. Soon as I walked in the door, Cameron saw me. He yelled, "Watch us, Mama B!"

He turned and asked Brandon, "Can you turn on the music so my great-grandma can watch us practice?"

"We don't want to spoil the surprise, do we?" came from Brandon.

I shrugged, set my back against the wall. "I don't mind seein' it more than once."

Brandon looked at the boy working with him. They got a kind of funny look on they face. "Okay. Here we go."

Cameron and his little friends stood in a row, backs to me. Then the music started and the boys got to steppin'. This time they didn't miss a beat. Clappin', slappin' hands, hoppin'. Whew! Tell you what, somebody oughta put them on T.V.!

I reckon the song they was dancin' to probably come from the world, but they cut out the words, so I couldn't rightly prove it.

Until they got to the chorus. Cameron and the rest clasp they hands together, press they index fingers and thumbs together like they got a gun. Man on the song say, "Pull out the forty-two, pull out the forty-two, pull out the forty-two."

Forty-two!

Before I knew it, I was in Brandon's face. "Did I interpret this right? You gon' have these boys pretendin' like they got guns? In the churchhouse, too?"

He bent down and pushed a button to turn off the music. Took a step back and said to me with a half-laugh on his face, "Ma'am, it's not what you think."

"Well, then, explain to me what it *is*?"

He started talking with his hands. "It's like a weapon of warfare."

The other young man working with Brandon started sniggering, like I can't see him out the corner of my eye.

"I done read all the weapons Christians use, and ain't nary one of 'em a gun. Who gave y'all permission to use this song?"

Brandon said, "We've used it at our old church. Really, I mean, the song is what you make of it. You can think of it as a gun, or you can think of it like…Matthew chapter forty-two."

The other young man nearly doubled over in silent laughter. *These boys must think I'm an old fool.* "Maybe I could *think* of it like Matthew chapter forty-two if there *was* a Matthew chapter forty-two."

I grabbed Cameron's hand and escorted him and Rosetta's boys back inside the sanctuary and straight to the vestibule. I turned them over to Nikki, asked her to take the other boys home and get started with Cameron's nightly routine.

Fear flashed across her face.

"Chile, go on. Ain't nothin' gon' happen to you in my house." I shooed her away.

My next step was to wait for Rev. Martin and Rev. Dukes. Mother's Board or not, this talent show was bound to be a bunch of mess with folk like Brandon headin' it up. Got my great-grandson actin' like he carryin' a gun. That's the *last* thing little black boys need to be practicin' for. We got enough problems in our community without the church addin' to 'em.

Rev. Martin and the good preacher was the last ones to the front, seein' as they got to lock the doors. Evidently, Brandon had already got to them before I did 'cause Rev. Dukes started the conversation with, "Hello, Mama B. Brandon tells me you had some concerns about the boys' step routine."

Push the mad out, keep the love in. Push the mad out, keep the love in. "Rev. Dukes, these boys plannin' to perform to a song about a gun, and act like they totin' guns in the show."

I saw the smile on his face just as stupid as the one on Brandon's. "There's nothing to fear. You know, a song is whatever you make it to be in your mind. And I think you're missing the point of this youth rally. We're going to bring in kids from this area who wouldn't normally find themselves at a church on a Friday night. Let them perform in a safe place rather than on a street corner. Feed 'em a hot dog and chips, send them home at a decent hour."

My head cocked to one side. "They gon' get fed any word here?" I knew when I said it, it was a stupid question. He ain't bit mo fed the grownups the word, so I knew he wasn't gon' give it to the kids.

Rev. Martin asked, "Would you feel better if we did it in the fellowship hall rather than the sanctuary?"

I got to give it to him. He tried to compromise. Some things don't need to be compromised, though. "Rev. Martin, the church *ain't* the world. We not out to compete with the world—playin' music glorifyin' guns, dancin' like we on a music picture show. What's the difference between us and a nightclub? Free hot dogs?"

Rev. Dukes put his hands up. "With all due respect, Mama B, you've got to understand things are changing. We have to do things differently to reach this generation. We have to try new stuff."

As wrong as I thought he was, I could hear how sincere Rev. Dukes was. He meant every word he said, from the bottom of his heart. So I said to him real calmly, "Son, it's one thing to entertain kids, another to raise 'em up with a heart for God. Kids don't need a bunch of new stuff. They need *true* stuff, the message of Christ, if you want to make a difference in they lives past Friday night."

A little vein popped out in Rev. Dukes head. Guess he got tired of talking to me. "The talent show will go on as planned. Good night, Mama B."

And he walked out the church with Brandon's crew trailing behind.

Me and Rev. Martin was the only ones left. I stepped outside the church doors, waited on the deck while he locked all the switches.

"Rev. Martin, I know Rev. Dukes some kin to you all, but right is right and wrong is wrong. And you know Pastor Phillips wouldn't go for this foolishness."

He fiddled around with the padlock longer than he had to. "Listen, I know what you're saying, but Rev. Dukes *is* family. His heart is in the right place, and he does know the way. I think he's just off on a prosperity tangent right now. I don't want to blacklist him."

I agreed, "Nobody tryin' to blacklist anybody. We just tryin' to—"

"Between you and me, I don't believe Pastor's wife is going to hold on much longer. Once she goes on home to glory, Pastor will be back and Mt. Zion can get back to normal."

Sounded like a coward move to me. Still, I couldn't be too mad at him. Just a few hours earlier, I felt the same way. Until I saw what Brandon had in store for my grandson. Made me think not only about Cameron, but about everybody else's little boy fall under Brandon and Rev. Dukes' guidance.

"I know Pastor left you in charge to keep everything going smooth. You got to recognize, good heart or not, family or not, Rev. Dukes doin' more harm than good right now."

Rev. Martin sighed, stared down at me with tired eyes. "Mama B, I got this, okay?"

Chile, I know when a man get a certain look on his face, ain't nothin' else you can say to him. He done heard all he can hear at the moment, and he shuttin' down so he can go process what you done said. Best thing to do in that point is shut-up.

"Night, Rev. Martin."

"Good night. I'll watch you until you get in your house."

"Thank you."

Chapter 23

One more thing I know about when a man gets like that: ain't nothin' else you can do aside from gettin' down on your knees and askin' God to do what you can't. So, that's exactly what I did when I got home. Got in that groove I done made from my elbows sinking in the mattress. Prayed to the Lord not only for Mt. Zion, but for Rev. Dukes' regular church and all the other ones that must be going off track. Chasing the things of this world. Forgetting to take the cross over while they tryin' to crossover. Just done forgot about Jesus altogether.

My heart got heavier the longer I prayed. Thought about all the violence in the streets, the ungodly influences our boys under. How they gon' learn the truth if they under leaders who don't read the word? Preachers who ain't disciplined enough to sit up under the Holy Spirit and let Him teach them how to divide the word rightly?

I also told the Lord I didn't plan on going to that talent show. Much as I loved Cameron and wanted to see him perform, I couldn't support him in what I felt was wrong-doing. I knew Nikki looked up to the Dukes so much, she wouldn't agree with me.

Made me sad I had ever insisted she come to Mt. Zion, considerin' the current state of affairs.

Then I listened. Waited for Him to tell me my part; if He wanted me to do something else in addition to fastin' and prayin'.

Started searching through the scriptures, thinking about all the times the people of God fought for the church. And when I landed in second Chronicles, I realized the Lord had decided to answer me in His word.

I like ta fell out laughin' when I saw it 'cause seem like every time I get myself all worked up over something, the Lord have to come in and remind me I ain't runnin' nothing. This ain't about people hatin' on me, like Rev. Dukes said.

This battle never belonged to me in the first place. It was His.

Chapter 24

Libby helped me practice how I was going to explain to Cameron about not going to the talent show. At first, I wasn't gon' say nothin', but I know how much he was looking forward to me being there. I didn't want him distracted by looking for me in the audience.

"Be sure and tell him you love him," Libby said.

"Got it."

"And ain't nothin' against him," she reminded me.

"I got that part already," I said. We was near the end of our walk, and I was near the end of my extra breath. No time for repeatin' stuff.

Time we got back to my home, we saw Cameron sitting in the living room crying, Nikki hugging him.

"What's wrong?"

"They're thinking about canceling the talent show tonight," she informed me. "Apparently, you're not the only one who's kind of upset about how things are going."

"Oh," was all I could say. Whatever the Lord was putting on the other peoples' hearts wasn't my fault – that's His doing.

Nikki gently pushed Cameron off of her. "Cameron, go to our room. I need to talk to Mama B."

I turned to Libby. "I'll see you later."

"Alright."

She left out while Nikki stormed off to the kitchen. I followed behind Nikki, ready to listen to what she had to say.

Nikki put one hand on her hip and the other on the counter. Guess she called herself about to give me a piece of her mind. "Cameron and his friends have worked very hard for this talent show. And they've gone door to door getting support. They've sold a lot of tickets, too."

"Tickets?"

She bucked her eyes out. "Yes. V.I.P. tickets. For people who want to sit on the front rows at the church."

"This the first time I ever heard of such!" *Lord, have mercy!*

"Well...Cynthia told me you wouldn't be happy about it. So I didn't say anything."

I bobbed my head up and down. "She's one hundred percent right that I'm not happy about it. And what's the money goin' to?"

Nikki lifted her shoulders. "I don't know. I guess the church."

Well, ain't that something? Gon' give up the front pews to the highest bidders. Wonder where they expect me and the rest of us who ain't payin' a red dime to get into our own church to sit. "Nikki, I hope they do cancel this talent show. This thing got trouble written all over it."

"How can you say that? It's just a bunch of kids singing and performing in church."

I shook my head. "I wish y'all would stop saying 'performing' anyway. 'Posed to be praisin' at church. When they gon' decide?"

"Rev. Martin said he'd call us back and let us know for sure," she said.

"Well, far as I'm concerned, it's canceled for me. I ain't goin' to the talent show even if they do have it."

Nikki's mouth dropped open. "Are you serious?"

"Yes, and let me explain why." Even if I wasn't going to speak my mind to the whole church, I needed to let my own granddaughter to understand. "Nikki, I believe the Dukes are sincere in their desire to help people. But they're sacrificing the truth for what's popular, and that's not right. So, no. I won't be coming to the talent show."

Suddenly, I heard a shuffling sound behind me. Cameron.

"Mama B, you're not coming to the show?"

Real slow, I turned to face him. I knew he wouldn't understand, which is exactly why I didn't want it to come out like this. That 'ole devil! Author of confusion.

I walked toward him, put a hand on his shoulder. "Cameron, I love you and I'm so very proud of all the hard work you done with the stomp group. But I don't believe God will be pleased by the dances Brandon done taught y'all. So, no. I won't be there."

I tell you, that boy started boo-hooin' like a two-year-old in need of a nap. Nearly broke my heart.

And it didn't get no easier once Cameron took his shower and got all dressed up for the show. Had on all black, like one of those—whatchama call it?—Ninja, some kind of turtles, I think.

"You look mighty handsome, Cameron," I told him, sitting on the couch in my lounging clothes.

He wouldn't even look up at me. "Thank you."

Nikki walked into the kitchen and peeked out the window. "Go on over to the church, Cameron. I see some cars already over there."

He skipped out the back door. Nikki watched him until he entered Mt. Zion, I presumed. Then she came back to the den and stood over me. "You sure you won't be there?"

"Nikki, I done already explained where I stand on this and why." I walked back to the den, flipped on the television and let it play. Didn't matter what was on the screen, my mindwasn't studyin' no show anyway 'cause my spirit was doin' flips inside my body.

She followed me like a lost, hungry puppydog. "Are you for real? How can you do this to Cameron? Do you have any idea how much he adores you?"

My face twitched as she went on.

"Every night since we moved here, when he and I pray together, you are the *first* person he mentions to God. Especially last night, when he asked God to make you come to the talent show."

"Well, Cameron's old enough for you to teach him that he has to pray the will of God, not just what he wants."

She tightened the corners of her mouth. "I can't believe this is happening."

Kept my focus on the screen ahead.

She grabbed her purse. "Alrighty, then."

Now that they was both gone, I turned off the tube, headed back to my room. Tried to pray, but for some reason, felt like I couldn't. So I paced through the house, from the front door to the back. Wasn't eatin' 'cause of the fast.

Wasn't like me. Wasn't like Him, either. *What's wrong, Lord?*

And clear as a bell, I heard one word in my Spirit: GO.

I knew without the whole sentence He was talkin' 'bout the talent show. I stood flat-footed in my den and asked out loud, "Lord, why You want me to go there? You ain't nowhere in that talent show."

Tell you what, my brain was doin' all kinds of jumping jacks in my head, busy and tryin' to figure out God's plan. How was I supposed to go over to the church and show my support for something so ungodly? So worldly? When Albert and I donated the land for Mt. Zion, we did it to glorify God and make His name great. Now, these folk want to use it for a infomercial and to mock His name? God forbid!

I paced through two more times before it hit me: my mind was no longer shakin', by then my insides had settled down. And God wasn't talkin' to me no more.

"Lord, do I *really* have to go?"

I know it don't make no sense to try and argue with God. He gon' win. Even if I half to look foolish while He does whatever He does.

And one more thing I know about God; He practice the Rule of One with me, too. He tell me something, He ain't gon' talk about it no more until I respond.

I walked back to the kitchen, looked through the curtains. Lot of cars in the church parking lot. More than we done had in a while.

Figured maybe I could sit on the back row. Come to think of it, I might not have a choice seein' as I didn't have a V.I.P. ticket.

Do I really, really, really have to go?

Why would He want me to go feast my eyes on such a hurtful sight? Had I been wrong this whole time about Rev. and Cynthia Dukes? Maybe they was onto something and *I* was the one off kilter.

Maybe my pride was the problem.

Whatever it was, I knew He would make it clear real soon.

"Lord, I don't know why, but at Your word, I'm going to that talent show."

Chapter 25

Queesha, one of Henrietta's grandbabies, met me at the door. Guess she was supposed to be some kind of usher. She always been a sweet girl, though. Met me with a smile. "Mama B, I heard you weren't coming."

I clasped her hands into mine. "Well, I'm here, sweetie."

She bit her lower lip twice. "I'm sorry, but all the seats on the front rows are taken."

"Don't mind me, Queesha. I'll just take a seat near the back."

Queesha's eyes apologized again. "You sure?"

"Yes. I don't know how long I'm gon' be here." Soon as the Lord give the word, I was gettin' out of there, you hear?

She pushed open the swinging doors to the sanctuary, and I had a flashback to the time when the church was overflowing with people – back before Peasner started growing and they paved the roads back into Dallas. Shoulders touching in the pews, choir standin' full, extra chairs set up down the middle row. If nothing else, the Dukes' knew how to fill a sanctuary with people.

They was all singing a congregational hymn, getting things started. But as I scooted onto the last row, my stomach started bubbling. I hadn't ate nothing but tea and soup for the past two days. Wasn't sure if it was my body or my Spirit trying to tell me something this time. And with all the different personalities flowing through the building, I couldn't be sure.

When I sat down good, here come the first act. I couldn't remember their names. Everybody just called them "the twins." Two teenage girls from Geneva side of the family. They got up singing somethin' with a church melody, 'cept the words didn't have nothin' to do with the Lord. Sound like two people ending a love relationship. Said, "Come to the end of the road" and "it's unnatural for me to be without you"—something like that. I couldn't hardly tell.

All the young folk got up, started swaying side to side, singing "Oooh!" when they got to the chorus part.

Didn't surprise me none. If Rev. Dukes don't preach the word, he sure don't mind folks not singin' 'bout the word.

Whole thing made me uncomfortable. But it was more than just them girls and all the people. And I wasn't sick.

By the second act, I put my finger on it: I was nervous. Something was off. Wrong. Not like theological wrong. Wrong in the spirit realm.

Brandon took the microphone again. "Ladies and gentlemen, we are about to bring out seven young men who are about to step for us tonight, and they are on fire!"

I thanked God Cameron was up next. Soon as he finished, I was out.

Brandon continued, "They call themselves the Lucky Seven Strikes. And they are—"

While he was talking, Cynthia come up and shoved him aside. "Excuse me, Brandon, I just want to say something before you bring out the next group of performers."

"No problem." He stepped aside.

Cynthia stood herself in front of the podium. She fanned over the entire congregation with her eyes. Then she stopped on me for a second. Give me a smug grin for a second. "I am so glad to see *everyone* here tonight. The *enemy* tried to keep this event from happening."

"Yeah!" the people said.

"Tried to stop the work of God from going forth!"

Folks stood up. "Yeah!"

"But I am here to tell you tonight, the work of God *will* go forth! No one can stop progress! You betta get with it or you *will* be left behind!"

My eyes stung. I knew good and well Cynthia had said all that on account of me. Why she couldn't just come up and talk to me one-on-one, I don't know. But it sure hurt my feelings something awful, I tell ya, for her to blast me out like that in front of the whole church. Left up to me, I would have been gone that very second.

She shoved the microphone back into Brandon's hand.

I shifted in my seat, pulled my purse in to my chest. Didn't have long to wallow in my own self-pity, though. The music for Cameron's dance come blaring through the sound system. And before they could even get started good, most the audience on their feet wavin' they hands, hollerin', "Pull out the forty-two! Pull out the forty-two! Pull out the forty-two!" Evidently, this one of they favorite songs.

For all the pride-swallowin' and lambastin' I endured, I couldn't even see my great-grandson perform. Too far in the back. And the folks on the rows in front of me had the nerve to stand up on the pews!

Wasn't no use in me standing up no more, so I sat back down. And soon as I did, somebody—a tall man with long nappy strings—come walkin' through the door. That nervous feeling went away. Now, anger. Like I just done seen my worst enemy walk through the door.

I followed the young man with my eyes as he made his way down the main aisle toward where Cameron and them was performin'. He got 'bout halfway up the way and I saw him reach into his pocket and take somethin' dark out.

Next thing I knew, everybody started hollerin' even louder, like they just saw something spectacular added to the show. "Pull out the forty-two! Pull out the forty-two! Pull out the forty-two!" they chanted.

And that's exactly what the man did. Wasn't until they heard the shot and saw the plaster fall from the ceiling they all realized his gun wasn't fake, and this wasn't part of the show.

Chapter 26

Everybody ducked down, started screaming. Folk on the back rows with me tried to crawl out the door.

Some of 'em got out before the gunman give an order into the microphone. "Nobody move! I didn't come here to hurt anybody."

Girl across the aisle from me sliding her thumb across her cell phone screen. Wouldn't be long before help got there, 'cause these kids can text faster than they talk.

"Nikki! Where you at?" the man yelled.

Nikki! Oh my God, help us. This got to be J.T.

Somebody crying.

"I know you in here!" J.T. shouted. "And you *betta* have my money."

Another shot. The sound of glass breaking. Light bulbs in a ceiling fan must have taken that bullet.

Somebody in the pews yelled out, "Man, we got about five Nikkis up in here."

J.T.'s angry voice boomed, "You want to be funny? Who said that?"

Close as I was to the ground, I could feel J.T.'s footsteps coming down the aisle. "Alright, you want to hide? Guess I'll have to shoot everybody in your section!"

That whole side the church squealed.

All of a sudden, I knew beyond the shadow of a doubt exactly why God had me come to the talent show.

Wasn't my own power, but His brought me up off that floor and onto my feet. And then I spoke. "Son?"

He spun around to face me. Gun in his right hand. Cordless microphone in his left. Sweatin' like he done smoked or drank something to get his nerve up for this mayhem.

"J.T., you don't have to shoot anybody."

He squinted, shook his head a bit. "Who are you? How you know my name?"

"I'm Nikki's grandmother."

"So you the one who's been hiding the fugitive? Well, you betta tell her to show her face before everyone in here get shot."

Somebody yelled out, "She in the front. Right side, in a red shirt."

J.T. looked around, but the view from where we stood didn't help him none. He couldn't identify Nikki, Cameron, or anybody else toward the front of the church.

He faced me again.

"I been prayin' for you, J.T."

"For what?" For some reason, he was still talkin' in the microphone.

"For the Lord to speak to your heart."

"Well, it's not working."

"Yes, it is. Prayers of the righteous availeth much."

Whew! When I said that, seem like something hit him dead in his gut. He must have recognized them words as something maybe his own Grandmomma said when he was a little boy.

"Don't pray on me no more, old lady." He was probably trying to sound like somebody he heard on TV, but I caught that little crack in his voice.

'Bout that time, I felt my Help comin' on. Closed my eyes, started speaking the word. "We submit ourselves to the Lord. We resist you, Satan, and you must flee."

Then Psalm 91 come flying out of my heart. "He that dwelleth in the secret place of the most High shall abide under the shadow of the Almighty. I will say of the LORD, He is my refuge and my fortress: my God; in Him will I trust."

Said it just the same as how I memorized it in Sunday school all those years ago. I took a peek with one eye and saw J.T. just standin' there looking lost. Paralyzed probably a better word.

"Because thou hast made the LORD, which is my refuge, even the most High, thy habitation; there shall no evil befall thee, neither shall any plague come nigh thy dwelling. For He shall give His angels charge over thee, to keep thee in all thy ways. They shall bear thee up in their hands, lest thou dash thy foot against a stone."

Ophelia stood up. She was on one of the back rows, also.

J.T. flipped around and stared at her.

She started speaking the word, too. "The LORD is my shepherd; I shall not want. He maketh me to lie down in green pastures: He leadeth me beside the still waters."

Me and her sayin' it together now. "He restoreth my soul: He leadeth me in the paths of righteousness for His name's sake."

At first, the prayer was just a whisper in the building. Then, heads started popping up. We got louder. Louder. "Surely goodness and mercy shall follow me all the days of my life: and I will dwell in the house of the LORD for ever."

We started the twenty-third Psalm over again. More and more people joined in, got up and faced J.T. He standing there frozen by the word.

Chile, the Spirit of the Lord fell so thick in that building, you could reach out and touch it. My, my, my. Never seen nothin' like it before.

Red and blue lights flash throughout the sanctuary. Police.

By this time, we shoutin' the Lord's prayer at J.T.

"Y'all crazy!" he yelled back, dropped the microphone.

Tell you what, though, he didn't pull that trigger another time. Boy got so confused, he rushed out the front door and turned himself in to first man in blue he saw. They say he begged them to take him away from the church!

Ooh, Lord, once J.T. ran outside, I nearly collapsed back on the bench. I think we was all in shock for a minute.

The police come in, ask if everybody else is okay. My throat was so dry, I could barely mouth the word, "Yes."

Folks started scrambling to get out the building. Nikki and Cameron run up to me shaking and crying.

Cameron hugged me. "Mama B, you were so brave. I was afraid J.T. was going to shoot you."

"You wasn't the only one."

"I'm so sorry," Nikki apologized to me over and over again.

Seemed like all night she kept on telling me how bad she felt she brought J.T. into my life, into the church.

Later than night, I finally sat down on Debra Kay's old bed and told her it wasn't all her fault. "J.T. to blame. He made the choices he made. But I got to tell you, we didn't help none by calling a forty-two into the sanctuary through that song they danced to."

I motioned toward Cameron, sleeping on the cot. Hmph. People handle trauma in different ways. Guess it must have wiped him out.

Her bottom lip fell. Astonished. "I thought…it was just a song. We didn't mean it."

"Devil don't care if you *mean* it or not. He want you to think it don't matter what you say, what you hear, what you read, what you watch on TV. He want you to think it's all fun and games while he programmin' your mind to all that foolishness, openin' up the spirit realm to his work."

I tapped her nose with my index finger. "He smart. A worthy opponent. And sneaky, I tell you. He like a woodrat. Get in your soul-house through any hole he can find. You can't give him no space – not through your eyes, your ears, your mouth – nothin'."

She hugged me again. I could still feel her heart beating fast.

"It's okay, Nikki-Nik. You safe. Always have been." Rubbed my hand up and down her back. Rocked her a little.

She sniffled. "I don't know what would have happened if you hadn't come to church tonight."

"Me, either. And I don't want to know."

We sat there in silence for another minute. Then she said, "Oh, I forgot to tell you earlier. I got a job offer. Cameron and I should be out of your hair in another week or so."

"Bless the name of the Lord." That should have been good news, but a part of me got sad. Almost two months since they showed up on my doorstep. I was gettin' used to company around the house.

Nikki bolted up, like she suddenly remembered something. "Mama B, did you feel…*it*…in the church tonight?"

"What?"

"*It*. Felt like…electricity or something. When we all started saying the twenty-third Psalm."

"Honey, that was the power of God."

Chapter 27

My emotions was so high, I couldn't sleep. Stayed up in the rocking chair crying, thanking God. Humbled He had used me in such a mighty way.

So I was up when I got the call from Pastor at two twenty-seven a.m. Geneva had passed away. "I'm so sorry, Pastor."

"Thank you, B. For everything. Geneva loved you so."

"Yes, and she loved you, too, Pastor." Now wasn't the time to let him know that his wife was ready to go. But some day, those words might be a comfort.

"You need us to come to the hospital?"

"No, no. They already done moved her body. Her sister is here. Rev. Martin, too."

"Yes, sir."

My body finally conked out around ten in the morning. Had to turn off the phone 'cause folk kept calling to see if I'd heard about Geneva. Then they would talk about the marvelous thing God had done at the church through me.

Henrietta one of the first ones to say, "B, we would have *all* been dead if it wasn't for you standin' up to your granddaughter's crazy boyfriend!"

Wouldn't be long before the whole town of Peasner had an exaggerated version of what happened at the church. Hard to exaggerate something much more than what actually happened, though.

Me and a few other church leaders met later in the day with a contractor. He looked at the holes in the ceiling, gave an estimate that sounded reasonable to us. We didn't have time for a whole lot of biddin' with the funeral on the way and all. They put up a tarp for the time being, said they'd be back to do the job first thing Monday morning.

I tell you what, though, Sunday, we praised God like we knew Him. He had done spared all our lives. This was one time I felt like runnin' around the sanctuary. Not for money, not for my haters, but for the goodness of God and the faithfulness of His word.

By the time Rev. Dukes got up to preach on what we all reckoned would be his last Sunday, I figured he wouldn't have to say much. We was already on fire.

He got up on to the main podium. Face all long, though, like somethin' troubling his heart. "Saints and friends, I have to repent."

Gasps all over the church house. "My wife and I want to repent."

Cynthia stood up, swiping tears from her cheeks.

"For the past weeks, someone in this church has been trying to warn us. Trying to tell us the importance of preaching the word. Preaching something that will stick to your spiritual bones. But we wouldn't listen. And how many of you know a warning comes before destruction?"

"Mmm hmm," we all moaned.

"Mama B, could you please come here, front and center?"

Took me by surprise. I looked to my left and my right like I didn't know who Mama B was. Cynthia come grab my hand, led me to the front with her.

Rev. Dukes come out the pulpit, stood right in front of us. "Mama B, all this time we've been here, you told us we needed to implant the word of God in the people's hearts. Not simply a love for things, selfish ambition, drive without direction, jubilee without Jesus. But Friday night, when the enemy walked right into this building, the only thing that mattered was the power of the word of God."

His eyes filled with tears. Cynthia's, too. Mine, three. I didn't want them to have to learn the lesson this way, but God knew best. I had no doubt He would use them like never before, after this.

They got it now.

After his sermon, entitled "Getting back to Jesus," Mt. Zion took up a big love offering for Rev. Dukes and Cynthia. They was so touched by our outpouring, they turned around and sowed it right back to the church.

Now I *know* they got it!

Cynthia give me the biggest hug after church. Invited me to come speak to their women's group whenever I wanted to. "Every time I left you house, you'd say something that kept me up all night. I might not have liked what you said at the time, but the Lord was working on me. Thank you for speaking the Truth in love, Mama B, and for being a true Titus 2 woman."

"You welcome, Sweetie. You take care." And we gave each other holy kisses.

After all the fellowshippin', me, Nikki, and Cameron walked on back to the house.

Chile, that big 'ole man sitting at my kitchen table almost took the wind out of me. "Son?"

"Hey, Mama. I didn't mean to scare you."

"Son!" I wrapped my arm around his neck. "I am so glad to see you."

He hugged me back, too. "I got your letter, and I did some thinking."

The very fact that he was sitting my kitchen let me know he must have agreed with me. On the inside, I was just a-gigglin' 'cause it tickles me every time the Lord answers a prayer by movin' on somebody's heart—and that person got the nerve to think they was the genius who changed everything. I tell you what, though, the prayers of the righteous done performed many a heart surgery, without the patient even knowing.

I stepped aside so Son could get a good look at his daughter.

Son cleared his throat. "Hello, Nikki."

"Hi."

Look like they needed my help. "Y'all can hug, if you want to."

Worst hug I ever did see! Like they two porcupines afraid they'd stick to each other. Still, it was a hug. *Thank you, Lord.*

I waited a second for Nikki to introduce Cameron, but the tears in her eyes told me I'd have to do the talking for her. "Son, this here is Cameron."

"Who's he?" Cameron asked me.

"This is your grandfather."

Chile, the biggest smile come on that boy's face. "My paw-paw?"

Son shrugged. "If that's what you want me to be."

Cameron slid into Son like a drawer in a cabinet. And somehow, Son's chest got big as a rooster at the same time.

Nikki was still standin' there with her arms crossed. Still mad. Still hurt. She needed some time. One thing I know about daughters, though: they might stay mad at they momma's for years, but something about they Daddy. He be the *first* one they forgive.

"Son, you gon' stay and eat with us?"

"Yes, ma'am."

The sound of the doorbell made us all stop.

"You expecting someone?" he interrogatin' me.

"No." I slid my apron back off. "Probably just somebody from the church. I'll get it."

All I could see through the peephole was flowers. "Who is it?"

"Delivery."

On a Sunday. "Deliverin' what?"

"Flowers."

Call me slow that day, but it took me a minute to put two and two together. I opened the door, took the bouquet of lilies from the man. Signed my name on the sheet.

"Thank you, ma'am."

"No, thank you."

Who on earth done sent me flowers?

I opened the card.

B, so sorry for the loss of your dear friend. Take care. –Frank Wilson

My goodness. Flowers.

I set them on the coffee table, stared at them for a minute. Smelled them. First time all year I'd had a chance to smell any because…well, because Albert's hadn't bloom for me.

Guess sometimes flowers bloom in unexpected places.

Son, Nikki-Nik, and Cameron washed up and joined me at the table for a pasta dish. New recipe I found on my iPhone. Son and Nikki didn't have too much to say to one another for now, so I carried the conversation while those two took turns stealing glances at one another. Trying to see themselves in one another. Takes time.

But you know Cameron didn't catch on to none of it. He was too busy stuffing his face. "Mama B, this is so good!"

"Thank you, Cameron. I'll have to remember this recipe for the next time you all come to visit."

Son said, "He's right. You put your foot in this, Mama. You've got to let me know when you cook this for Cameron again."

I grinned at my child's round-about way of sayin' he wanted to see his daughter and grandson again. "I sure will, Son. Sure will."

The End

Want More Mama B?

You got it, chile!
Here's an excerpt from *Mama B: A Time to Dance*
Book Two in the Award-winning,
Bestselling Mama B Series

Chapter 1

Pastor Phillips sure was lookin' good and strong up there in the pulpit again. Hadn't been but a few months since our first lady passed away, but the Lord was restoring Pastor Phillips the same as He did me when my Albert died. It takes a while, but after the one you done shared a bed and a life with for forty something-odd years dies, it's hard to sleep at night again. We do the best we can to get settled. Can't get too settled, though, 'cause at our age, we know it won't be long before it's our time to go, too.

I was sixty-four when Albert died. Eight years and five months ago. Some time, seem like it was just yesterday, though, especially if I get to thinking 'bout it too hard. So I don't. Albert wouldn't want me to spend what little time I got left feelin' sorry for myself.

Besides, I assure you, Albert Jackson, Sr., is not up in heaven moping around about me. Knowing him, he probably ain't even asked Jesus if I was coming up soon. Too busy asking David and Paul all those questions he had about the Bible. Whew – that Albert could talk your ear off!

Yes, Albert was something else.

And so was first lady Geneva Phillips. She sure gon' be missed.

Soon as service was over, you couldn't beat Henrietta skating herself up to the pulpit to talk to Pastor, standing by his side while he greet the visitors. Good Lord, it was a shame the way that woman threw herself at him. She got to be at least three years older than me, carrying on like she need special prayer from Pastor.

She need special prayer, alright. Pray herself right on back to the altar and into the baptism pool!

Lord, I'm sorry.

Nevermind Henrietta, I rushed out the church and across the lawn through the gate to my own back yard. Had to hurry and transfer the pulled chicken simmering in barbeque sauce to a proper Tupperware bowl. Once I'd packed that up, I wrapped up a few rolls in foil, scooped a couple of servings of baked beans into another bowl. Finally, I scraped half the pan of peach cobbler aside for myself, kept the other half in the original throw-away container and slapped some plastic on top.

I set all that in a paper shopping bag and headed back over to the church to give it to Pastor. I knew if he was anything like me, he'd been lost about things his spouse used to do. That Geneva could cook up a storm, too!

"Here you go, Pastor," I said to him as I transferred the handles from my hand to his. He and Reverend Martin were just locking up the front doors by then. "Chicken, beans, and peach cobbler."

"B, you don't have to keep cooking for me," Pastor said as he stooped down to give me a thank-you hug.

All I could think was how much it hurt inside to go home to an empty house the first few years after Albert died. I was hoping the food might take Pastor's mind off the loneliness at least a teenchy bit.

"Pastor, I'll take Mama B's cooking if you pass it up," Rev. Martin stuck out his hand like he was intending to take the sack.

Pastor Phillips swatted the hand away. "You gon' fool around and draw back a nub."

"I'm just saying," Rev. Martin laughed. He looked better, too, now that Pastor had returned to the pulpit. No more visiting ministers preaching all kind of foolishness, scattering the flock in different directions.

Henrietta come hopping out of her car. Fast as she whipped out of that front seat and scrambled back to Pastor's side, I don't see how she ridin' around with handicapped license plates.

"Pastor!" She flagged with her handkerchief as she shuffled her way into our conversation. "I got some ice cream to go with that peach cobbler. I can have my niece bring it by your house later on this afternoon."

"Oh, no, Mother Henrietta, that's alright. I can't take in too much sugar at once."

Henrietta pursed her lips for a second. "You sure? It's Blue Bell."

"That's mighty tempting, but I'll have to let it go this time. God bless you for thinking about me, though."

Lord knows, if I was the gossiping type, Henrietta sure would have gave me plenty to talk about. But I ain't the one to talk about people, so I don't. Just keep it between me and Jesus.

She waddled on back to her car while me, Pastor, and Rev. Martin stood there and watched just what way she was backin' out so she wouldn't hit none of us. Once she was clear, we said our good-byes and promised to pray for one another until we met again.

The rest of my Sunday I spent watching football. One thing I don't like is people talkin' during the games, so I do my very best to watch football at home alone. And that's exactly what I did until the last second of the last game.

Nothing like a good 'ole Cowboy game and some peach cobbler.

I tell you what, whoever this is knockin' on my door after nine o'clock at night better be some kin to the late Ed McMahon.

"Just a minute!" I wrapped my robe around my waist and pulled the belt to. Good thing about these old houses, don't matter what size you are, your feet make you sound like Godzilla walkin' across these hardwood floors. Make strangers think somebody real big on this side of the door. "Who is it?"

"It's Derrick, Mama B."

"Derrick who?" I set my ear up against the door so I could catch his voice maybe.

"Roy James and Winona's son."

Lord, what Derrick want at this hour? I twisted both locks to the left and beheld a sight for sore eyes. Derrick LeVon Jackson, my nephew from my husband's side. Might as well have been my grandson as much time as he spent at this house with my grands, especially during the summer.

"Well, to what do I owe this pleasure, if that's what it is?"

I hugged him, felt his heart racing even through his shirt.

"Hello, Mama B. It's so good to see you."

I stepped back and pointed him toward the couch. The clock showed it was nine-thirty. In my book, might as well have been midnight, but I know the young folk don't think the same. "You hungry?"

"No, thank you."

He sat down on my sofa, letting a black duffle bag fall at his feet. I already knew where this was going, so I started praying. *Lord, I don't know what the problem is, but he sure can't stay here while he find the solution.*

I hadn't been too long getting back into my routine after my granddaughter and great-grandson, and Cameron, moved out. They had stayed with me most of the summer while Nikki found a new job and closed the door on a relationship with her deranged ex-boyfriend.

Somebody must done put out the rumor that my house was the Red Cross. *I don't think so, Jesus!*

Chapter 2

I sat down across from him and we made some small talk. He asked about me and mine, I asked about Roy James and Winona. Derrick said they was doing fine in their retirement village in North Dallas. He said it was almost like a cruise ship, they had so much to do in the complex.

If I wasn't so busy with the church and the food pantry, I might give one of those places a second glance.

Soon as I found a lull in the conversation, I decided to cut to the chase. My word, it was going on 9:45 by then! "Well, I know you ain't stopped by here just to catch up on me. What's the matter?"

He dropped his head. Look like a cloud of shame come over his whole body while he tried to fix his lips on the first word to say.

"Go on and spit it out."

He exhaled. "I messed up."

Couldn't help but chuckle. "Join the club, son. I been president a time or two."

Derrick shook his head. "No. I mean I *really* messed up. I don't know if my life will ever be the same, or if Twyla is going to take me back. It's complicated, Mama B. I just need a place to stay for a little while."

Don't take no genius to figure out his problem got something to do with another woman. This is exactly the kind of business I keep my nose out of. "Well, I'm sorry to hear you two are having problems, Derrick, but y'all got to work this thing out." I stood up so he could get the signal it was time for him to leave.

"But I can't stay...at home," he said, with his behind still flat on my couch.

"I didn't say you had to go home. All I'm sayin' is you can't stay *here*. I don't house no marital fugitives." I crossed my arms.

Derrick grabbed the short handles of his bag and rose. "I understand, Mama B. Where's the nearest hotel?"

"Down Main, left on Second."

"Got it."

"I'll be praying for you and Twyla."

He raised one eyebrow and sucked in his cheeks. Seem like every man on my husband's side of the family got that same expression when they got no clue of what to do. "I don't know about praying. I doubt God wants to hear anything from me right now."

"Oh, He'll listen. You might not like what He has to say about it, but He will listen because He said He would," I assured Derrick.

"Good night, Mama B. Thank you."

"Anytime. Well, make that any time before eight, you hear?"

We shared a laugh as he walked out the door.

I made good on my word. Went back to my bedroom, got on my knees and prayed for him and Twyla. They hadn't been married but five years or so. Had a three-year-old daughter, Kionna, cute as a button. *Mmm*, mmm, mmm. I know the devil is busy tryin' to tear up families. Don't help none when folk make foolish choices. But if the truth be told, we all done something we knew we had no business doin' at least once upon a time.

Lord, I don't know what Derrick did, but You do. I bring him, Twyla, and that precious baby before you. Not because they've done everything right, but because You are good. I intercede on their behalf. In Jesus' name, Amen.

I tried to call Winona, but her voice mail picked up. I left her a message letting her know Derrick and Twyla might need some help by way of prayer. Me and Winona go way back. She know how to keep things between me and her and God long enough for Him to work it out. Plus, she's his Momma. We got a way of praying for our kids that God pays special attention to, I believe.

When I got up off my knees, I rolled back in bed. I had just snuggled up under the covers when that same knockin' come on the door again.

My goodness! Folk gon' think I'm runnin' numbers up in here with all this nighttime traffic!

I stomped back to the door, knowing it had to be Derrick again.

Chapter 3

"Mama B," he said before I had a chance to fuss at him, "please. I went to the hotel but...I can't stay there."

"What you mean you *can't* stay there? It's a free country, last I heard."

"Even if I could stay there, Twyla's got the credit cards."

He let his eyes drop to the floor again. I knew that was a half-truth if I ever heard one. No wonder he got caught doing something. Derrick was a terrible liar.

But for the first time, it hit me: Derrick really was sorry about whatever shenanigans he'd been up to. This thing would work itself out eventually. In the meanwhile, however, he was only asking for a place to rest his head which, I suppose, is better than asking for money.

"Boy, you betta thank God I'm led by the Holy Spirit. Get on in here."

"Thank God and you, Mama B!" Derrick grabbed my neck a little too eager-like.

"Wait just a minute here! We gotta come to an understandin'," I piped up. Now, I let Nikki stay here for free, it's true, but I can't bring myself to let no able-bodied grown man stay under my roof without paying something. God ain't in that arrangement.

Derrick stepped back, still wearing a boyish grin. If memory served me right, he wasn't too much older than Nikki, which would put him in his late twenties. Too old to be babied, too young to put him out in the streets if I didn't have to.

"You workin' right?" I checked.

"Yes. Got a good job in Mesquite, not too far from here. I won't even be here during the day."

"Mmm hmm. Rule number one, rent is a hundred dollars a week."

"Yes, ma'am." Derrick quickly reached into his wallet, flipped it open, thumbed through, then slapped five twenties in my hand. I guess he figured he'd better give me the money before I changed my mind. "What else?"

"No keepin' up racket all night. No other woman in this house except your wife if she comes to visit you. Church every Sunday at ten o'clock sharp."

"Yes, ma'am."

This boy cheesin' like he done won the lottery.

"How long you plan on staying here, anyway?"

"I wish I knew, but it's really out of my hands."

It ain't outta mine. "We need to sit down this time next week and get some timeframes in mind."

"Yes, ma'am."

I took a deep breath and let it out. As much as I wanted to fuss at Derrick about whatever it was he did, I couldn't. Wasn't no good in makin' my guest feel uncomfortable during his visit. Whatever his problem, he already felt bad enough. "You can stay in Son and Otha's old room."

He followed me down the back hallway so we could get him set up with fresh sheets and towels. I bit my tongue the whole time 'cause Lord knows I wasn't in the mood for no more houseguest. *Why me, Lord?*

Then the Holy Spirit brought a memory to my mind, fresh and clear like it was just yesterday. I remembered standing on the front porch, holding hands with Albert as my old pastor and Deacon Handley dedicated this house to the Lord. Hmph. Every once in a while, the Lord'll have to remind me that everything I got belongs to Him. Wasn't for Him, me and Derrick might be in the same boat.

As we forced the fitted sheet to grab hold of the bottom of the mattress, I started humming to the tune of "I Surrender All." That song sure is a lot easier to sing than to do, I tell you.

"I forgot about your singing," Derrick smiled.

"Hmm?"

"You used to sing and hum all the time." Already, he looked lighter. His face was a perfect blend of his parents. Roy James' tight eyes, Winona's broad nose. Almost all the cousins, my kids included, had inherited a dimple in the chin. This trademark had become near and dear to my heart. Derrick was family. I needed to remember that, too.

"Oh, yes, I sing all the time." I smiled back. "Gets me through the day a lot easier."

He froze and gave me a smart-aleck smirk. "You sound like my Momma. Both of you are *retired*. What's so hard about life at this point?"

"There's more to life than work, I'll have you know. I got my friends, my church, and my family with people like *you* that need lookin' after."

He laughed again. "You got me on that one, Mama B. You got me."

We finished fluffing the pillows on the bed. "That oughta do it."

Derrick stopped for a moment and looked around the room. He nodded. "Man, I used to want to be like Son and Otha. They had it made."

"So did you."

"Naw, not like they did. They had every new video game, new movies, new scooters. Y'all had everything. I used to love coming over here."

Come to think of it, he was right. We were blessed beyond measure. "Well, God is good."

"I guess so," Derrick said.

"Oh, honey, I know so. Goodnight."

"Goodnight, Mama B. And thank you. You won't be sorry."

"Night, Derrick." *I surely hope not.*

Other Books by Michelle Stimpson

Fiction

A Forgotten Love (Novella) Book One in the "A Few Good Men" Series
A Shoulda Woulda Christmas (Novella)
Boaz Brown
Divas of Damascus Road
Falling into Grace
I Met Him in the Ladies' Room (Novella)
I Met Him in the Ladies' Room Again (Novella)
Last Temptation (Starring "Peaches" from *Boaz Brown*)
Mama B: A Time to Dance (Book 2)
Mama B: A Time to Love (Book 3)
Mama B: A Time to Mend (Book 4)
Someone to Watch Over Me
Stepping Down
The Good Stuff
Trouble In My Way (Young Adult)
What About Momma's House? (Novella with April Barker)
What About Love? (Novella with April Barker)
What About Tomorrow? (Novella with April Barker)

Non-Fiction

Did I Marry the Wrong Guy? And other silent ponderings of a fairly normal Christian wife
Uncommon Sense: 30 Truths to Radically Renew Your Mind in Christ
The 21-Day Publishing Plan

A Note from the Author

This Mama B series has sparked a new desire to fellowship with believers and share the gospel in the same ways Mama B does—not by preaching at people but by letting Christ be known in the way I treat others. I pray that her example of a godly woman will encourage you to think about how you want to be after walking with the Lord for 40+ years.

If you have yet to start your journey in Christ, let me encourage you to seek Him. Seek Him in all of his glory, all of His love, and His wisdom. If you feel the tug in your heart, Thank Him for His goodness, ask Him for forgiveness, and invite Him to live in you. He stands knocking on the door of your heart and is more than pleased to come in and be your Lord (Rev. 3:20). And as both Mama B and I can testify to, He is a good Lord indeed!

God bless you!
-Michelle Stimpson

About the Author

Michelle Stimpson is the bestselling author of more than 25 books and 50 short stories. Visit her online at www.MichelleStimpson.com.